Marrying Mandy

Brides of Clearwater Book 1

Melanie D. Snitker

Marrying Mandy
(Brides of Clearwater Book 1)
© 2018 Melanie D. Snitker

Published by
Dallionz Media, LLC
P.O. Box 6821
Abilene, TX 79608

Blue Valley Author Services
www.bluevalleyauthorservices.com/

For permission requests, please contact the author at the e-mail below or through her website.

Melanie D. Snitker
melaniedsnitker@gmail.com
www.melaniedsnitker.com

This is a work of fiction. Names, characters, businesses, places, events, and incidents either are the products of the author's imagination or used in a fictitious manner. Any resemblance to actual persons, living or dead, or actual events is purely coincidental.

ISBN: 0-9975289-6-6
ISBN-13: 978-0-9975289-6-1

For my grandma, Amy Shults.
From peppermint tea and
magical holidays as a child,
to my graduation and wedding,
you've always been there for me.
I am blessed to be your granddaughter.
Much love always!

Prologue

Eleven Years Ago

Fifteen-year-old Mandy Hudson lifted her chin and squinted. Sunlight filtered through the canopy of the maple tree creating a kaleidoscope of colors. A gentle breeze mixed the scent of soil with sun-warmed leaves. She took in a deep breath. This was one of the many things she loved about her grandparents' land.

A voice drifted down from the tree above her. "Are you coming up or not?"

She tossed a glare at her friend, Preston Yarrow. At sixteen, he enjoyed teasing her and liked to boast about his climbing skills. He'd dared Mandy to join him on the branch at least twenty feet off the ground. Mandy had no doubt in her ability to ascend to his level. She just couldn't do it nearly as fast. Then again, those crazy long legs of his gave him quite the advantage.

"Hold your horses." Maintaining three points of contact, Mandy picked her way through the branches until she was sitting on the same thick limb where

Preston waited, watching her. With one arm wrapped around the trunk, she shifted until she was comfortable, her other arm resting on one knee.

From where they sat, they could see her grandparents' home, the Hudson Bed and Breakfast. Sun made the nearby river glitter as if someone had sprinkled diamonds across the surface. Grass and trees stretched as far as they could see.

Once Mandy had her balance, she let go of the tree trunk. The bark left grooves in her palm, and she picked off a piece of debris.

Preston's gray eyes reflected the blue sky. His dark blond hair had lightened after a summer of spending time outdoors in the sun. Mandy swore he'd grown two inches in the last year and now seemed to tower over her when they stood side by side. He looked thoughtful, almost sad, as he scanned the view below them.

They sat in comfortable silence until he spoke, his deep voice filling the surrounding space. "I'm going to college when I graduate. Then one day, I'll own a place like this."

He'd been saying that regularly for years now. She shot him a teasing look. "You're going to run a bed-and-breakfast?"

He countered her tease with an exaggerated scowl. "Funny. No, I want to build like your grandfather does in his spare time. Except I want to turn it into a business."

Papa had spoken highly of Preston's skills when it came to woodworking. Mandy gave him a smile. "I hope you find a place like this and all your dreams come true." She took in the beautiful view around her. "I can't imagine living anywhere else."

When her parents had divorced and started new lives, they'd happily signed away their rights and left Mandy behind. Their ability to disregard their eleven-year-old daughter like yesterday's paper had broken Mandy's spirit. Her grandparents gave her the love and time her parents never had. Moving to the Hudson B&B had brought her the loving family she desperately needed, not to mention a friend in the boy who'd mowed the lawn and helped Papa since Preston was twelve.

Preston glanced at the watch on his wrist. "I'd better get back to work. Mr. Hudson wanted me to help him repair part of the back fence that blew loose with the last storm." He grasped the limb he was sitting on and swung himself down to the one right below. He continued to make his way to the base of the tree.

She followed him, landing on the grass-covered ground with a grunt. She dusted off her shorts and held a hand above her eyes to block out the sun. "I don't know how you manage all of your homework with as many hours as you work here."

He shrugged. "I'm saving every penny. I'll need it to buy land and build my own house." He focused on her face and grinned, his eyes lighting up with mischief. "One day, I'll have a wife and spend every day building on my own land."

He'd always had his future lined out while Mandy was lucky to think further ahead than next week. She chuckled. "Sure. And where do you think you'll find all that?" When he didn't answer right away, she looked up at him again. He shifted, allowing his height to block the sun for her.

He held her gaze, his expression serious. "The house and land? I have no idea. I'm pretty sure I already know who I'm going to marry."

She took a few moments to fully grasp his meaning. Her eyes widened and she gave a quick shake of her head. "Well, I'm never getting married. My parents and their messed-up lives taught me that."

Preston raised an eyebrow as though he considered her statement a challenge. Without hesitation, he leaned in and gave her a quick peck on the mouth. She'd barely registered the feeling of his warm lips touching hers before he pulled back again.

"Never say never, Mandy." With a playful wink, he took off toward Papa's workshop which was situated behind the house.

Mandy planted her fists on her hips. The nerve of him! She touched a finger to her lips and ignored the way her cheeks heated as she realized she'd received her first kiss.

It didn't matter.

No one would change her mind about marriage, and that included Preston Yarrow.

Chapter One

Preston knew the moment Mandy walked into the sanctuary. Hushed voices became even quieter, except for Mrs. Whipple who didn't bother whispering when she said, "There she is. Bless her little heart."

Several people offered their condolences and gave Mandy hugs or pats on the back. She returned them all. Both Mandy and Preston had practically grown up in Clearwater Community Baptist Church in Clearwater, Texas. It was natural for so many people to express how sorry they were for the loss of Mandy's grandmother, Samantha Hudson.

Preston could tell by Mandy's tight jaw and wide eyes she was barely keeping it together. He left his seat next to his parents, stepped into the aisle, offered her his arm, and motioned behind him. "I saved you a spot."

Mandy followed him in, taking the seat to his right. Everyone else took their cue and found their own places before the memorial service began.

Mandy adjusted the skirt of her black dress. She

looked uncomfortable, shifting several times before clasping her hands in her lap. It was only the second time he'd seen her wear a dress. The first was at her grandfather's funeral almost a year before. Preston had done yard work for Barry Hudson since he was a kid, and the man had been a force to be reckoned with. Mr. Hudson had taught Preston everything he knew about gardening, repairs, and woodworking. It was that last subject Preston had enjoyed the most as he spent hours watching Mr. Hudson craft fences, furniture, and even small boats by hand. Preston couldn't imagine missing his own grandfather more, and still felt the loss keenly every day he continued working at the Hudson Bed and Breakfast.

Mandy picked at her left thumbnail, and Preston resisted the urge to reach for her hand. Dealing with her grandfather's death last year had been hard enough. But with her grandmother gone... Well, she was alone now. And she'd made it clear she wanted no one to get overly sympathetic with her. She looked down at her hands, her straight, dark brown hair acting as a curtain to hide her face.

Preston's parents, Stanley and Ellen Yarrow, sat to his left. His mom leaned over and whispered, "I hope she'll be okay. I still can't believe Samantha's gone."

All he could do was nod his response. Mandy would be okay, but it wouldn't be easy for her.

By the end of the memorial and graveside services, Preston easily detected Mandy's weariness even if no one else seemed to be aware of it. Mandy continued to thank everyone for coming, never once letting her emotional control slip.

The muggy mid-September afternoon fit right in

with this unusually warm fall. Sweat dampened Preston's shirt as he waited, back to a tree, until he and Mandy were the last two people in the area. When her shoulders sagged, he pushed away from the trunk and stood next to her. "You all right?" She shrugged. "Dumb question, huh?"

"Maybe. But what else is there to say, right?" She stared, unseeing, at her grandmother's grave. "At least they're together again."

The newly dug grave would soon be blanketed with grass like the one next to it. Preston thought about the way Mr. Hudson would've welcomed his wife in heaven and smiled. "Mrs. Hudson was never the same after he passed."

"No, she wasn't." Mandy swallowed hard and blinked several times as though trying to keep tears at bay.

Preston didn't remember the last time he'd seen her cry. Had he ever? He knew she was determined to stay strong, a fact she'd harped on many times in the years they'd been friends. But it wasn't healthy to bottle up emotions like she did. "You know, it's okay to cry. No one will fault you for it. I certainly wouldn't." He'd shed tears himself at the loss of two such important people in his life.

"Uh-uh." Mandy crossed her arms in front of her and straightened her spine.

"Why not?"

"Because if I start crying, I may not quit." Her deep brown eyes shifted to his and begged him to understand. "I'm alone now, Preston."

"No, you're not. I'm still here."

He silently prayed she'd find the strength to make it through this. It wasn't fair. The poor woman had suffered more loss than anyone ought to deal with. Well, he wouldn't let her face it on her own. No matter how much she insisted on doing exactly that.

Before he died, Mr. Hudson asked Preston to keep an eye on his girls. Considering Preston had been in love with Mandy since he was fifteen, it was an easy thing to agree to. He had every intention of continuing to fulfill that promise.

~*~

It wasn't even six Friday morning and Mandy stood in the kitchen at a complete loss. After having closed the B&B for the last week, she'd opened the place back up for business. They had guests scheduled to come in this afternoon. Even though people had cautioned her about going back to work two days after the funeral, she needed to stay busy. Besides, the place had been struggling financially since Papa died, and Mandy couldn't afford to turn down the business.

The back door swung open and Jade Wilkes came in. Her graying hair was pinned up in a tight bun, and she frowned. "I wanted to check on you this morning. Honey, you should wait another week. Everyone would understand." She engulfed Mandy in a hug. Her honeysuckle-scented perfume tickled Mandy's nose. Jade had cooked breakfast at the B&B for years and always claimed it to be her second home.

Mandy steadied herself after being released from the suffocating embrace. "I can't. We have reservations, and I refuse to cancel them."

"Then you'll want me to be here like usual tomorrow to cook up breakfast?"

"Yes, please."

Customers often mentioned Jade's amazing meals in reviews. B&B repeat customers raved about her breakfasts. The older woman perused the thick recipe book that always sat on the island. Granny never put it away because she was constantly in the kitchen baking something. If it wasn't chocolate chip cookies to hand out to the guests, it was blueberry muffins for Mandy.

At the realization Granny would never again bake her a blueberry muffin, Mandy's heart gave a painful twist. This place wasn't the same without her grandparents. She'd do everything she could to keep the B&B running like they'd want her to, and that meant there was no time to feel sorry for herself. She'd done plenty of moping around when she was a kid, and it hadn't gotten her anywhere.

Jade jotted several things down on a slip of paper. "I'll swing by the store and pick up a few supplies. How do homemade bagels and an omelet bar sound?"

Normally, the thought of Jade's omelets would make Mandy's stomach growl and her mouth water. But today, she had to swallow past her dry throat and her thick tongue. "That'll be great, Jade. Thank you."

"Absolutely." Jade patted her on the arm, a sympathetic expression on her face. "I'll see you bright and early tomorrow."

Mandy waved goodbye. The moment the kitchen door closed, she sagged against the counter and let out a slow breath. The key was to keep as busy as possible through this long day. If she could do that, maybe she could banish to the back of her mind the pain of no longer having Granny there. "God, how am I supposed to do this without them?" No answer came, only more of the same hollowness in her chest.

When guests stayed at the B&B, there was always something to do. But, for the moment, everything was under control in that department. Jade would have food covered for tomorrow. And Elise Johnson said she'd be in at her normal time to clean and make sure all three rooms were fresh for the guests. Granny had hired her two years ago to come every morning to clean them and do any other related chores around the house as well. Both women had been friends of her grandparents for years.

After Papa died, Granny just didn't seem to care about maintaining the B&B like she used to. Elise had taken over more cleaning than normal to help out. Mandy was thankful. While she was at the house all day, she had a long list of clients who paid her to build and maintain their websites. That was a full-time job all on its own and, frankly, the income from that was what kept the B&B running.

Then there was Preston.

He'd been helping Papa with repairs, yard work, and more since before Mandy had come to live with her grandparents. Preston was probably out there somewhere right now, working his magic. He usually stayed on the property until lunchtime. At that point, he left for his job at the local lumberyard.

Before Papa died last year, he took care of anything else that needed attention the rest of the day. Now, Preston came back in the late evenings to deal with any problems. Granny had called him only if it was an emergency, and Mandy intended to follow suit. She didn't know how the poor guy fit everything in during the day without wearing himself out.

Mandy depended on Preston, and she couldn't imagine her grandparents' place without him. Preston was a good friend and a huge blessing in her life.

She normally stayed indoors during the morning, helping Granny bake or taking care of phone calls and managing the B&B's website. In the afternoon and early evening, she'd handle everything her web clients needed. The place was way too quiet without Granny. Echoes of what used to be—the laughter, teasing, and joy—were gone. The house echoed like an empty shell, and it drove Mandy crazy.

By nine, she was over the quiet and the memories that kept encroaching on her attempts to focus on other things. She headed outside. Preston tended to the landscape, but surely he wouldn't care if she watered the flowers growing in the bed along the front of the house.

The moment Mandy crossed the threshold and stepped foot on the large covered porch, she sucked in a breath of air as though she'd been deprived of it until near suffocation. Her eyes slid closed. She focused on the breeze as it played music in the trees nearby while birds sang songs to each other. The familiar sounds brought her comfort. Grounded her.

Out here, she could pretend everything was the way it used to be. Papa was in the workshop putting another coating of sealant on his newest project. Granny was inside making those strawberry scones everyone loved. And Mandy was right where she needed to be: home.

Unwilling to let that go, Mandy picked up the end of the hose, turned the water on, and began to soak the gorgeous flower beds Papa had spent years cultivating. Colorful roses the size of Mandy's palm, Texas sage, and firewitch welcomed the spray. Marigolds, pansies, petunias, and other bright flowers joined the shrubbery, creating the beautiful sight that welcomed guests to the Hudson Bed & Breakfast.

Mandy had been watering the flowers for a while when Preston rounded the corner of the house, a pair of work gloves tucked under one arm. When he saw her, he altered his trajectory and came to stand next to her.

"I'd have taken care of that."

Mandy nodded. "I know. But I needed something to do." She hedged a look at the front door of the house as though something dangerous might lurk inside.

Preston's gray eyes studied her until Mandy let her gaze return to the shower of water. Other than her grandparents, Preston knew her best. She'd never been able to hide her emotions from him—something that had irked her growing up.

He motioned to the flower boxes. "These need to be watered every morning. You'd be doing me a favor if you wanted to take it over. You can always tell me if things get too busy and you need me to go back to watering them myself."

"I'll see to it they're taken care of." Mandy looked at him out of the corner of her eye. She thought he would say something else before he hesitated and closed his mouth again.

Preston finally motioned behind him. "I'd better get back to work. I should have everything done by eleven, then I may spend a little time in the workshop if that's okay."

She released the trigger on the spray nozzle, stopping the flow of water, and turned to face him. "You never have to ask for permission to use the workshop, Preston. Papa loved it when you worked in there. I think—" Her voice cracked, and she swallowed. "I think you were the grandson he never had." She ran a hand through her hair and pushed it away from her face. "Losing Granny doesn't change that."

"Thanks, Mandy." He rested a warm, calloused hand on her arm. "Remember you're not alone. I'm praying for you. My parents are, too."

When she avoided his gaze, he leaned over to make eye contact until she nodded. "I appreciate that."

Preston's thumb brushed across her arm twice before he let his hand drop. With a last comforting smile, he turned and headed toward his truck in the driveway.

Mandy went back to watering flowers. She still felt his hand on her arm. How was it possible a simple touch from Preston made her heart pound in her chest like she'd just finished running a marathon? It was maddening.

Preston Yarrow had had a way of affecting her since the day she met him. She'd done her best not to let him know it, though. There'd been a time when she'd had a schoolgirl crush on him, a devastating prospect to a girl whose life and family had been ripped apart by her parents' infidelity and inability to put their family first. Mandy had long ago decided she wouldn't give her heart to a guy. It wasn't worth it, not after all she'd seen.

She'd been able to push how she felt about Preston into the shadowed recesses of her mind. But every once in a while, at times like this when he reached her in ways no one else could, she wished things were different.

Chapter Two

Preston lifted the last of the concrete blocks into the back of the black pickup and closed the tailgate. He turned to the woman purchasing the heavy load of supplies. "They'll ride fine until you get home. I hope you have someone to help you unload all of that."

She smiled. "I'll be waiting for my dad and brother to come over tonight."

"Sounds like a plan. You have yourself a blessed day, ma'am."

"You, too. Thanks again."

She climbed into her truck, and Preston took the push cart back to the front of Clearwater Lumber and Supplies. He parked it with the others and entered the air-conditioned building. Sweat dripped down his back due to combining ninety-two-degree weather with heavy lifting. The day fall weather truly hit would be a welcome one. He stopped in the breakroom to get a long drink of cool water before wandering back to the checkout lines.

Preston had a variety of jobs at the lumber store where he'd worked for the last eight years. He could handle almost anything they needed him to do. Most of the time, though, he either carried things into the store, or hauled them back out for customers.

Thankfully, that meant he didn't need to go to the gym, which was good, because between his full-time job and working for the Hudson B&B, he didn't have much spare time.

Mandy came to his mind again, and he said a silent prayer for her. She'd seemed lost this morning, and it nearly broke his heart. She seemed to refuse to grieve, and while he knew it was never easy to lose someone so beloved, he worried that she wouldn't be able to heal.

He hoped things went smoothly today and there weren't any emergencies requiring him to return to the B&B when he got off work. At the same time, an excuse to check on her would be nice, especially since tomorrow was Saturday and he didn't normally go to the B&B during the weekend unless an urgent situation came up. Maybe he'd call Mandy tonight or tomorrow and make sure she was doing okay.

He felt a little better with the decision and went to help a customer load up a large order of lumber—something that proved challenging given the size of the vehicle. But he got it all arranged, pulled his gloves off his sweaty hands and tucked them under his arm, then went back inside in search of more water.

The rest of the evening dragged. It wasn't nearly as busy as a usual Friday thanks to the new big chain home improvement store that opened a block away almost a year ago. Ever since their grand opening, business at Clearwater Lumber steadily dropped. Preston, along with his coworkers, hoped to see things improve soon. After all, Clearwater was a small town of almost twenty-five thousand people who usually looked out for their own. But apparently, the cheaper prices and bigger selections of the larger store trumped even that loyalty.

Preston kept busy moving some of the new plants to their places in the garden center until Chet, one of his coworkers, approached him, a look of apprehension on his face. "Mr. Logan wants to see everyone up front as soon as the doors close."

Preston's brows rose. An all hands on deck meeting? Not good. He swallowed his concerns. "All right. I'll be there." He checked his watch. Fifteen minutes until the nine o'clock closing. He finished up his current task and made his way to the front of the store.

Team members, some in uniform and others in street clothes, leaned against check-out counters or visited with each other. Clearly, many employees had driven in specifically for this meeting. The second Mr. Logan approached, everyone became quiet.

Preston already suspected bad news, and the regret on Mr. Logan's face confirmed his misgivings.

Mr. Logan hooked a thumb through one of the belt loops of his pants. "Hey, everyone. I called and invited as many employees to come for this meeting as could make it. The rest I'll call tomorrow." He paused and frowned. "As you all know, my daddy opened this store back in the 1940s. I grew up working here, and it's been a privilege to follow in his footsteps and keep this place running for the good people of Clearwater." He swallowed. "Despite my every attempt to do so, we can't keep up with our newest competitor."

He didn't need to specify which business he referred to. Everyone else nodded as murmurs of agreement and even a few unkind words filled the air.

Mr. Logan held up a hand to stop the chatter. "I have no choice but to sell this place and move forward. It's the last thing I want to do, but I've been offered a price that's more than fair for the property and the building. Over the next two weeks, we'll be placing everything on sale to liquidate the inventory."

Everyone suddenly seemed to talk at once. Chet turned to Preston. "I knew this was coming."

Preston sighed. "Yeah. Seems like it was inevitable." He turned his attention back to Mr. Logan.

"Unfortunately, it also means I'll have to let y'all go. Consider today your two-week's notice. Clearwater Lumber will close its doors the Saturday after next." Mr. Logan looked like he was firing family members. In a sense he was, as he'd known a lot of these people, Preston included, for most of their lives. He folded his arms over his chest. "I'm sorry, y'all. If there was anything I could do, you know I'd do it."

Several people asked questions which Mr. Logan did his best to answer. The fact no that one took their anger or disappointment out on their employer spoke to the fairness with which he'd always treated those who worked for him.

They were all assured their normal schedule would remain for the last two weeks.

"What are you going to do, Mr. Logan?"

The question came from Cindy. Everyone stopped talking, all gazes trained on the man whose eyes had widened.

"Well, my wife insists it may be time for retirement." He barked that husky laugh everyone associated with him. "I don't know if I'll be able to do that. Maybe I'll finally get around to writing the great

American novel I've always wanted to write." He winked at them.

Preston chuckled. Truthfully, though, he worried about Mr. Logan. The guy had worked non-stop since he was a kid helping his dad. He deserved to retire in comfort, but with the economy the way it was anymore, it was getting harder and harder for people to do that.

His thoughts shifted to his own father who struggled every day to bring enough money in. Preston had seen his parents fight for everything they had and still not come out on top. Preston had spent his life caught in the same struggle.

And now one of the two jobs he relied on for everything was coming to an end. No, neither job was what he'd envisioned himself doing when he was a kid, but they paid the bills, and he didn't hate them.

Especially working for Mr. Hudson at the B&B. Except now he worked for Mandy.

It'd be nearly impossible to find another job with an employer who would understand his time commitments to the B&B. The thought that he might have to give that job up made him feel sick.

He'd cross that bridge when he came to it. The time would go by fast, but for now, he had a two-week reprieve. One thing was certain, he had no intention of breathing a word of this to Mandy. The last thing she needed was yet more stress on top of everything else she was dealing with right now.

~*~

"Thank you, Preston." Mandy watched as he finished installing the new doorknob on one of the guest rooms. "I couldn't believe it when Mr. Palo had to call me and tell me they were stuck in here." She might have found the whole thing amusing if she weren't so exhausted. It was only Monday, but it seemed much later in the week.

"Did you move them to a different room once you got the door opened?" Preston tested the knob and then turned to face her.

"I did. They're staying through today and going home tomorrow. Thankfully, they had a great attitude about the whole thing. I gave them a gift card to Terry's Diner for lunch. That's where they are now." She had to admit she preferred the quiet when her guests were gone. That was not always the case, but right now, she'd rather not have to fake a smile or chit chat.

"Are you pretty booked?"

Mandy frowned. "We don't have nearly as many reservations as I'd like." Having guests at the house constantly could be exhausting, but it was good for business, and it helped keep her too busy to think about much else. The lack of reservations meant that not as much money was coming in and she had way too much time on her hands. "Everything going okay for you so far this week?"

Preston hesitated before moving to place the screwdriver back into his tool kit. "Same old thing. Work and more work." He gave her one of the winks that always had other ladies in town swooning.

Mandy refused to let those winks, or anything else Preston might throw at her, affect her in the same way. Ever since the day he'd kissed her under the tree, she'd made sure he knew she was *not* going to get involved with him or anyone else.

But there was something in his gray eyes

suggesting he wasn't being entirely truthful. Things weren't always easy at home, especially since his dad's kidney transplant six years ago. Last she'd heard, Mr. Yarrow's health was stable. "How're your parents doing?"

"They're good, thanks."

She still thought he was avoiding something. "I'm here if you need to talk."

One corner of his mouth hitched upward. "I appreciate it, Mandy."

The sound of the bell at the front door echoed upstairs. Mandy threw Preston an apologetic look and hurried down the narrow stairs. She'd expected to see a delivery of something, or a new customer inquiring about a room. The man in a smart business suit carrying a briefcase made her pause. "Can I help you?"

"Are you Mandy Hudson?"

"I am." She stuck a hand out. "And you are?"

He took her hand and gave it a firm shake. "Brock Walters from the Walters Brothers Law Firm. We're located on Rosewood Street. Perhaps your grandmother spoke of us?"

Mandy nodded. "Yes, of course. She mentioned you a time or two." Preston came downstairs and paused. He gave her a pointed look, and she returned it with a little shrug.

Brock introduced himself to Preston, who returned the gesture, as they shook hands.

Mandy cleared her throat. "What can I do for you, Mr. Walters?"

Brock approached the oak table and set his briefcase on it, popping open the lid and reaching inside for the papers.

Preston moved to stand next to Mandy, a gesture

she appreciated. Did Granny have debts Mandy didn't know about? She doubted it. Then again, she hadn't anticipated a lawyer walking into the B&B, either.

Brock held two pieces of paper at an angle making it impossible for Mandy to catch a glimpse of what they might contain. "We've managed the assets of both Barry and Samantha Hudson for years. They've been specific about their will and what they wanted to happen to their assets once they passed on."

Mandy bit the inside of her cheek. The way he said it sounded cold and rehearsed. Her grandparents—the only real family she had—were dead. She didn't care about assets. They wouldn't bring her grandparents back to her.

Preston must've sensed the rabbit trail her thoughts had taken. He took a side step, allowing his arm to brush hers, and stayed there. Normally, Mandy would have moved to put distance between them, but right now, she needed the reassurance his touch was providing her.

Brock continued. "There are some things related to Mrs. Hudson's will I'd like to discuss with you. Would a meeting tomorrow morning at nine work for you?"

Mandy blinked at him. What did he have to tell her that he couldn't say right now? Her curiosity was piqued as was her anxiety. "I think so. I'll need to speak with someone to cover for me, but it shouldn't be a problem."

"Perfect." Brock turned his attention to Preston. "How about you, Mr. Yarrow?"

That seemed to surprise Preston, and he looked at Mandy before responding. "I'm sorry?"

"There is business with you regarding the will.

Unless you'd rather come to the office separately. That can certainly be arranged." Brock pulled his phone out of his pocket and opened the calendar application.

Preston spoke hurriedly. "No, tomorrow morning at nine will be fine for me as well."

Brock smiled for the first time since he'd introduced himself. "Wonderful." He handed each of them a sheet of paper along with a business card. "I'll need you both to bring at least two forms of ID listed on this paper to the address provided."

Mandy's eyes flitted over the information. "Any idea how long this meeting will take? I'll need to let someone know."

"An hour for this first one should suffice." Brock closed his briefcase with a snap, shook both of their hands, and headed for the door. "Thank you for your time. I'll see you both tomorrow."

Mandy continued to watch the door for several seconds after it closed, obscuring her view of the lawyer. "This first meeting?" she mumbled. "What on earth?" Her attention shifted to Preston.

He was studying the business card before he folded the paper and stuffed both into his back pocket. "I have no idea. You sure this guy's legit?"

"Yeah, they went to see him once a year, usually in January or so. I can't remember if Granny did this year, though." After Papa died last year, Granny changed a lot of the things she normally did. "I guess we'll find out tomorrow."

"Do you want to go over together? I don't mind driving. I'll be here, anyway."

Mandy thought about arguing but quickly acquiesced. "That'd be great, thank you." She had no idea what the lawyer was going to want to talk about, but there was no ignoring the ball of nerves in her stomach that seemed to be growing by the minute. What if there were debts she didn't know about? The whole place barely stayed afloat as it was. What if her mother decided to stick her nose into the whole affair? Ugh, why hadn't she at least asked the lawyer if her mother was going to be at the meeting as well? She hadn't seen her—or her father—in more than three years. It'd take a lot more notice than this to face either of them again. They hadn't even bothered to show up for Granny's funeral. She'd been angry for her grandparents, but relieved otherwise.

The touch of Preston's hand on her arm drew her out of the avalanche of emotions.

"Hey. It's probably procedure to get Mrs. Hudson's bank accounts transferred to your name and things like that."

"Then why do they want you to be there?" No matter which options Mandy entertained, none of them made real sense.

"I don't know. We'll go there tomorrow, hear the guy out, and move forward from there. No sense in borrowing trouble we don't need, right?"

He was still touching her arm, and Mandy resisted the urge to lean into him. "Right."

Was it ironic that the guy she'd managed to avoid getting too close to was the only person she felt she could rely on right now?

Chapter Three

Preston opened the door to the Walters Brothers Law Firm and held it for Mandy. Frigid air immediately blasted them. Air conditioning was a must in Texas for a good part of the year, but this was ridiculous. He noticed the goose bumps that immediately peppered Mandy's skin. "I have a jacket in the back of my truck if you'd like it."

Mandy rubbed her arms. "Please."

"Sure. Be right back." He retrieved it and then held it while Mandy threaded her arms through the sleeves. She pulled it closed in front of her and slipped her hands into the pockets. Preston hadn't worn the jacket in months. Hopefully, he'd left no tissues in the pockets. When she didn't react, he assumed everything was fine.

Brock Walters walked into the waiting area and motioned for them to follow him. "I'm glad you could both make it. A beautiful morning, isn't it?"

Preston and Mandy both muttered polite responses as he ushered them into a plush office. They each claimed a chair and waited until Brock walked around and sat in his leather seat.

It always amazed Preston how much he had to fight the urge to reach for Mandy's hand in situations like this. He glanced at her. She was sitting straight as a rod, her hands in her lap. She picked at her thumbnail like she always did when worried or stressed.

Brock shuffled papers around on his desk. "I want to tell you both again you're welcome to meet with me privately if you prefer."

Mandy looked at Preston. "I'm good."

Relieved, Preston nodded his agreement.

"Wonderful. Then we can begin." Brock found the paper he was looking for and then made eye contact with Preston. "Let's begin with the easiest part first. Mr. and Mrs. Hudson had a will drawn up together. Once Mr. Hudson passed, no changes were made and all stipulations within the will remain in place." He paused and took a drink from a bottle of water.

The continued delays were getting to Preston. He wished the man would just say what he needed to say instead of dragging things out. Maybe that was a lawyer thing to see how much he could make them squirm. He barely detected the sigh from Mandy and covered a smile. Apparently, she felt the same way.

Brock put the lid back on the bottle. "Mr. Yarrow, I have here that Mr. Hudson willed all the contents of his workshop to you." He paused for dramatic effect.

He didn't need to. Preston couldn't have been more surprised than he already was. His mind tried to grasp the meaning of the lawyer's words. He'd spent years helping Mr. Hudson in that workshop, building things for the B&B. Preston had learned everything he knew from the hours he spent watching Mr. Hudson craft boats or furniture. His dream for a future woodworking business was born from the time spent with his mentor.

Since Mr. Hudson's death, Preston had only gone into the workshop when necessary. The memories echoing through the large building were difficult to take most of the time. It wasn't the same without him.

He knew Mr. Hudson cared about him and had often referred to Preston as his adopted grandson. But to leave everything in there to Preston?

The sign of friendship and trust caused tears to sting the back of Preston's eyes.

What did Mandy think? He turned his head to catch her expression, happy to see the pleased look on her face. She gave him a little smile of encouragement.

Brock handed Preston a sealed envelope. "This is for you. I'd like for you to read it after you leave here, give all of this consideration, and then let me know your thoughts. If you accept the contents of the workshop, we can draw up those papers by the end of the week."

Preston took the envelope. It wasn't thick, yet felt weighty with the emotional ramifications of what might be inside. Even though he was curious, he knew he wanted to be alone when he read it. He tapped it against his watch and laid it across one leg.

This meeting already proved to be a surprise. Even though Mandy seemed to approve of the will up to this point, he'd want to talk to her and make sure there was nothing of her grandfather's she wanted to keep for herself.

Brock made several notes before looking up at Mandy. "Now, the part of the will pertaining to you, Miss Hudson, is more complicated. I assure you I double and triple checked these details with your grandparents, and Mrs. Hudson, especially, was adamant they were correct. I think it'll be easier if I read it aloud." He opened a file folder and scanned it. "In the event of their passing, Mr. and Mrs. Hudson have specific stipulations in place for the Hudson Bed and Breakfast as well as all property and land, the contents of the workshop not included." He paused here and Preston wanted to reach across and shake the man, especially if it meant he'd get on with it. "One of two things must be done with regards to the Bed and Breakfast and all property specified above. The first option is to put it all up for sale. It must be sold for the amount specified by an appraisal. All funds garnered from the sale will be immediately transferred to Mandy Lynn Hudson to be used as she sees fit."

Preston glanced at Mandy. She had her jaw clenched and her lips pressed together hard enough to turn them white. She wouldn't sell the property no matter what. She'd claimed it was a link to her childhood. Really, the only childhood she ever had. She'd hold on to that, tooth and nail. Preston searched his brain for another possibility for the other option.

The lawyer continued, oblivious to the emotions bouncing around his little office. "The second option is this. Should you, Mandy, become married by the end of this calendar year and remain married for at least one full year after that date, all titles to the B&B and attached properties and land will go to you specifically. At that point, it would be your decision whether your husband would be added to the title or not."

Mandy's face went white in shock.

~*~

She blinked at Brock and waited for him to correct himself or say something else. When he didn't, she got out of her chair and put her hands on the edge of his desk. "You've got to be kidding me. My grandparents would never put together a will like that. I don't believe it."

Brock came around the desk and handed Mandy a small stack of papers attached at the corner with a gold paperclip. "I assure you they did. You are welcome to contest the will. But I will warn you it'll cost money and you'll have to hire a different attorney. It is an option though. Please take your time reading these first and if you have any questions…"

Mandy woodenly accepted the papers and slowly read through the will. When she got to the part the lawyer had referred to, she read it twice. If she didn't know firsthand that both of her grandparents had remained sound of mind until their passing, she'd sure wonder after reading this. Mandy handed the will over to Preston who scanned the pages himself. She'd like to contest it, but knew there was no way she could afford the fees. She barely kept the place running as it was.

Mandy cleared her throat and rubbed a thumb across her forehead in an attempt to focus. "So, let me see if I understand this correctly. To keep the Bed and Breakfast I practically grew up in, I have to get married and stay married for a year? Otherwise, I'll be forced to sell it."

Preston glanced up from the will. "Would it be

possible for someone to buy it, then for Mandy to turn around and use that money to buy it back?"

"It would." Brock looked hopeful. "I can tell you there's been more than one interested party offering to buy the place over the last year or two. The B&B is situated on a highly prized piece of land."

That was true. Several people had offered to buy the whole kit and caboodle after Papa died. All of them wanted to tear down the Bed and Breakfast and build some kind of resort or a row of houses overlooking the Guadalupe River. Such a purchase would result in triple the money in return for the developer. Granny had been adamant about not letting the property go like that, and Mandy wasn't about to, either. What were the odds she could find someone who would purchase it and then be honest enough to allow her to buy it back from them again?

Preston held up the papers. "Can we get a copy of these? Upon Mandy's agreement, I'd like my lawyer to read through the will as well."

Mandy shot him an appreciative look. If Granny trusted Mr. Walters, she knew he was telling the truth, but she'd much rather have someone else examine the will. Maybe there was a loophole or something.

Brock retrieved the paperwork without hesitation. "Absolutely. Let me go make those copies for you right now." He disappeared, the office door closing behind him.

"What were they thinking?" The words passed Mandy's lips before she'd realized she'd uttered them.

"I'll talk to my cousin today and see if there's something you can work with." He paused and when Mandy looked at him, she could tell he was suppressing a smile.

"What?"

"This is way more eccentric than I thought your grandmother was capable of being. But she always insisted that, one way or another, you'd change your mind about marriage."

Mandy's face grew warm. He was right. Not only that, but Granny and Papa had both insinuated that Preston was half in love with her years ago. Mandy insisted they were wrong. She never dreamed Granny would go to this extreme to get her to change her mind about marriage. It was practically blackmail. "Well, I sure hope there's a way around it. I'm not giving up the B&B. I'll figure something out."

Preston's face grew serious again as Brock walked back in and handed Mandy a large envelope. Brock sat down and retrieved an envelope identical to the one he'd given Preston. "This is for you, Miss Hudson. It's from your grandmother. She told me it should answer all your questions. Again, please take it with you and read it in the comfort of your own home."

Her own home? According to the lawyer, at least as of this moment, she had no home. She took the offered item and tucked it into her bag. *Granny, you have a lot of explaining to do.*

Brock stood and placed his hands on the desk. "I suggest you both read your letters, think on things for a while, and then call me. I gave you both my business card. If you have any questions, don't hesitate to contact me by phone or e-mail. We can arrange another meeting next week to go over specifics once you've made your decisions."

That last part was directed toward Mandy. She grimaced.

Preston stood and Mandy followed suit. The next thing she knew, she was sitting in the passenger seat of Preston's truck. He stood at her door, his face filled with concern. "You okay?"

"Honestly? I have no idea."

He said nothing else as he drove them back to the B&B. Mandy was perfectly content to ride in silence as well. Once there, they both stood in the driveway as Mandy handed the large envelope containing the copy of the will to Preston.

"I'll ask my cousin, Jeremy, about it today. See if I can get these scanned in and sent to him before I get to work. I'll let you know as soon as he responds." His eyes wandered to the workshop.

"I appreciate it. And, hey, I think it's fitting Papa left all of that to you. That's how it should be."

Preston seemed to appreciate her words and smiled. "I sure miss him."

"It's not the same without him. Either of them." Mandy hiked a thumb toward the house. "I'd better get inside and make sure things are going well. Jade agreed to stay until I got back, but I'm sure she has somewhere else to be."

"All right. Don't work too hard today. Call or come find me if you want to talk about the will or anything else."

Normally, Mandy would've been happy to go inside. But right now, it surprised her that she'd much rather stay out here with Preston. She wasn't willing to analyze the realization to find out whether it was because she was escaping the emptiness of the house, or because she wanted his company. "Don't work too hard yourself. I'll see you later."

Except for the ticking of the clock on the wall

that read fifteen minutes after ten, the house was silent. Jade came around the corner and greeted her with a wave. "Did everything go okay with the lawyer?"

Mandy shrugged. "Lots of mumbo jumbo, you know how it is. I'll have a second lawyer look over everything this week."

"But she left you the B&B, right?"

"Yes, she left me the B&B." Mostly. Mandy had no intention of letting it go, and as far as Jade was concerned, it was remaining in the family.

Jade looked relieved. "Well, I'm real glad to hear it. The Palo family checked out. They decided to go tour the town a little before they headed for home. We have two different reservations checking in this afternoon. For now, all's quiet."

"Great. Thanks again for sticking around, Jade. You should be good to go."

They said their goodbyes, Jade retrieved her things, and Mandy was left by herself. Elise wouldn't be in until eleven, which gave Mandy plenty of time to read the letter from Granny.

Dreading the emotional storm reading the letter would stir up, Mandy kicked her shoes off, poured herself a glass of unsweetened iced tea, and headed for the living room. With her legs curled under her, she opened the envelope.

Even the paper smelled like Granny. Mandy closed her eyes and inhaled. If she concentrated hard enough, she could almost convince herself that Granny was beside her on the couch, ready to give some of her sage advice. But when Mandy opened them again, she was still alone. She felt the tears building up and refused to let them flow. Blinking them back, she read the flowing script.

My Dear, Sweet Mandy,

I'm writing this letter now knowing that, one day, Mr. Walters will have to give it to you. The selfish part of me never wants that to happen. You see, I know the day your parents left you here was one of the darkest days of your life. And it should have been. You should know it was also one of the brightest days for your Papa and me. Having you here has been nothing but a joy. We couldn't ask for a better granddaughter, and it's been a blessing to watch you grow up into a beautiful and thoughtful woman.

If I'm gone, you're likely feeling alone. I want to remind you that is never true. We'll always be in your heart. God is watching over you now like He always has. And don't discount Preston's friendship. You like to protest otherwise, but that young man cares a great deal for you.

You're probably wondering about my will by now and why I put stipulations into you owning the Bed-and-Breakfast. Honey, I want more for you out of life than what you're allowing yourself. I know you've sworn you'll never marry after what happened with your parents, but I can tell you marrying Papa was the best thing I ever did. You deserve that kind of epic love. The thought of you running the B&B alone for the rest of your life saddens me.

The B&B is important, but not nearly as important to me as you are. So, I'd rather you sell it and use the money to move and start over. Or, if you're determined to stay here and keep the place running, then I want you to reconsider marriage. Sharing your life with someone is important. And I'm sure we can both think of at least one young man that just might fit the bill.

Mandy's face heated as her mind immediately flew to Preston. Granny had spoken with her several times about how she shouldn't let her own parents' poor decisions color her view of marriage, but it was hard not to. Couple that with watching Granny's devastation when Papa died and could anyone blame Mandy for wanting to bypass all the pain and grief?

She swallowed hard and continued to read the rest of the letter.

All we've ever wanted was for you to be happy and to live a full life. Don't let the actions of the past anchor you. Allow yourself the freedom to sail away into the future. You may surprise yourself and find a treasure you never knew you were looking for.

Think about it and pray over it, Mandy. Papa and I love the B&B, but we love you more. If you choose to take the money, we will be no less happy for you.

Never doubt you are loved and cherished, my precious granddaughter.

Until we meet again in Heaven.

All My Love,
Granny

The handwritten letter swam in front of Mandy as tears gathered in her eyes. No! She hadn't cried when Papa died, and she didn't cry at Granny's funeral. She refused to weep now. Swiping at the moisture, she composed herself and blinked away the tears.

She hoped Preston's cousin would find a loophole in the will, but she had a suspicion there wasn't one. That was one thing about Granny: Once she made up her mind, there was no use trying to change it. If he were here, Papa would laugh and say Mandy had inherited that particular trait in spades.

Mandy knew her grandparents loved her. She

had to keep this house. It was full of their memories, and she wasn't about to let it go. Preston's face came to mind and her heart immediately pounded away beneath her ribs. Then she shook her head to clear her thoughts.

No. She'd been adamant against marriage, and this development didn't change anything. There had to be a way to save her grandparents' B&B that didn't include marrying Preston.

Chapter Four

Preston parked the riding lawnmower in the storage building and secured the door. With an hour until he had to start his shift at Clearwater Lumber, he reached into his back pocket and withdrew the envelope Mr. Walter had given him.

He took a steadying breath and walked across the yard to the workshop. Letting himself in, he turned on the overhead light and took a seat in an old wooden chair. The piece of furniture had more nicks and scratches on it than paint after years of sitting in what used to be a busy building. Preston had once asked Mr. Hudson why he didn't sand and refinish the chair.

Mr. Hudson had pointed to a big gash in the leg of the chair. *"You see that mark there, Preston? I was carrying out my first handcrafted canoe and ran right into it. And the red smudge? My beautiful wife came out to keep me company while painting her nails and spilled some polish. I got it off except for where it'd colored a section of the chair that was already dinged up."* He'd paused with a wistful smile on his face. *"This chair tells stories, my boy. I have no intention of forgetting even one of them."*

Preston ran a hand over the red mark. He'd tell Mandy about this chair and everything her grandfather said. She might want to keep the chair herself.

Focusing on the envelope in his hand, he straightened it out and tapped one end against his knee. He then tore the other end and slid the piece of paper free. The page was filled with Mr. Hudson's scrawls. He'd teased the older man about how his handwriting rivaled a doctor's in its illegibility. Preston smiled at the memory and read the letter.

Preston,

I've long valued your help around the B&B. I've also enjoyed your company in the workshop. Having someone to share in my interest has turned my hobby into something more. I've seen the way you light up when you work. I know this is something you'd like to turn into a career, and I know you could do exactly that.

I'm leaving the contents of my workshop to you. I hope you'll take this equipment, and the knowledge I've passed down to you, and you'll use it all to build the future you deserve.

Please know I'm not leaving all of this to you simply because you've worked for me for years. Or because you've been my protégé here in the workshop. I leave this to you because, as far as I'm concerned, you are my grandson.

I'm proud of the man you have become.

Papa Hudson

P.S. Do me a favor? Watch over my granddaughter for me, will you? Don't let Mandy fool you with her tough-gal exterior. You are her closest friend, and she needs you.

Preston read the letter over twice more before he

bothered to brush away a tear. A deep breath brought in the scent of cedar along with the memories the smell invoked. This place would never be the same.

But even as he mourned the loss of the man he considered his grandfather, hope took root. He looked around him, noting the different pieces of equipment he'd never dreamed of being able to afford before. If he could find a location to move all of this to, then just maybe...

Mr. Hudson wanted him to build a future, and that's exactly what Preston would do. He'd have to work through the logistics. It wouldn't be easy, but there had to be a way.

His mind swimming with numbers and possibilities, Preston realized he'd been sitting in the workshop for more than a half hour. He'd have to hurry to get to Clearwater Lumber in time. He was halfway back to his truck when he heard people talking in front of the house. Mandy's voice sounded strained. Preston jogged around the corner to see her standing in the doorway as though blocking the entrance. A man waited on the porch in front of her and didn't look like he was in a hurry to leave. With gel-slicked dark hair, shiny black shoes, and an expensive suit, he looked like a sleazy used car salesman.

Mandy shook her head. "I'm still not interested. If you'll excuse me, I have guests that need my attention..."

The man took a step closer to her. "I assure you, you will not get a better offer than this."

Preston didn't need to hear more. He walked up the steps of the porch. The sound of his shoes against the wood caused the man to turn and look at him. Preston didn't stop until he was standing next to

Mandy, never taking his eyes off the stranger. "Is there something I can help you with?"

The man's eyebrows lifted. "I'm speaking with Miss Hudson. I'm not sure it's any of your business."

That wasn't the right thing to say if he'd wanted Preston to back off. "The lady said she wasn't interested. I can assure you Miss Hudson is not someone who changes her mind on a whim. I suggest you take your leave."

With a fake smile that made Preston want to growl, the man pulled out a business card. He slapped it down on the railing of the porch. "When you change your mind, call me." He turned on his heels and stalked to his fancy sports car.

Preston didn't move until the man's vehicle had driven out of sight. He picked up the business card. Grayson Vincent with Vincent Land.

Mandy let out a forceful breath of air. "Thank you. He wouldn't take no for an answer."

"He wanted you to sell?"

She nodded. "He's been here for twenty minutes trying to convince me why his offer was the best and why I should sell today." Sparks of anger shot through her eyes as she stared in the direction he'd driven. "I may have no choice but to sell in order to buy this place back, but it won't be to him."

Preston pulled out his cell phone and took a photo of the business card before handing it to Mandy. "Tell me if he bothers you again. I wouldn't trust him for anything. I'm sorry you had to deal with that, he clearly had no tact."

"He's the third one." When she saw his surprise, she elaborated. "I've had two other companies call and offer to buy the B&B and the land." Her shoulders fell as she looked out over the sea of rolling grass between the house and the river beyond. "If I have to sell, how will I know which place to trust enough that they'll let me buy it back?"

Preston had no easy answers. If he had the money, he'd do that for her in a heartbeat. As it was, he barely had the funds to go month to month. His thoughts went back to the workshop. If he could come up with a plan, maybe that would finally change soon.

With more hope about his finances than he'd had in years, he gave her a reassuring smile. "We'll figure this out." He glanced at his watch. "I'm running late. I've got to get copies of the will off to my cousin and get to work. Why don't I call you later? If I hear back from Jeremy, I'll come by when we close up and we can talk about what he says. See if we can brainstorm some ideas."

He'd half expected her to object. Instead, the stress on her face lessened. "That would be great. Thanks, Preston."

"Of course. And I'm serious. Call me if that guy bothers you again."

"I will."

Preston said goodbye and jogged to his truck. He returned her wave and watched her disappear inside the B&B, his determination bolstered. Mr. Hudson believed in him enough to hand over the equipment to make his dream of a business possible. He also wanted Preston to look out for Mandy.

Preston wasn't about to let him down on either front.

~*~

The B&B had been so busy all day, it might as well have had a revolving door. Even though she knew Preston was on his way, Mandy still cringed when the front door opened, half expecting it to be someone else who wanted to buy the place. As soon as Preston appeared, she breathed a sigh of relief that must have shown on her face because he looked concerned.

"Long day?"

"Oh, yes." She ran a hand over her face as though it might wipe away the exhaustion. As pathetic as it sounded, she'd love to go to bed right now even though it was only nine o'clock. But with guests in the house, she rarely fell asleep before eleven if she was lucky, especially now that she was handling everything on her own. "Both families are still out by the lake tonight."

Preston held up the large envelope of papers. "Want to sit out on the back porch and talk?"

Her momentary mood lift from seeing Preston evaporated. She locked the front door, turned the sign to say everyone was around back, and led the way. The light near the back door flooded the red-stained oak porch. Papa had built it himself. She still remembered when he and Preston had restained it a couple of years ago.

A flurry of bugs dive-bombed the light. Mandy opted for the stairs and Preston joined her. In the distance, they heard the voices of some of the guests along with several peals of laughter from one of the children. The sounds brought a small smile to Mandy's face. It reminded her of the many evenings she and Preston would run around the yard, chasing after fireflies. Mandy once tried to fill up a whole jar with them, convinced they would light her way back to the house. She'd been disappointed when Granny said she couldn't keep them at her bedside.

Mandy's gaze landed on the envelope now resting on the step between them. "What did your cousin have to say?"

"Jer looked the whole will over and even consulted with one of the senior partners at the firm. The will is ironclad." He shrugged. "I was hoping he'd tell me about a loophole in there somewhere."

"Yeah, me, too." Mandy leaned to her right against the railing running down along the steps. Even with the light shining behind them, she could still pick out the stars as they began to appear in the sky. "I can't lose this place, Preston."

"I know." He said nothing else for a few moments, and they sat in silence. "If I could afford to, I'd buy this place from you in a flat second. You'd buy it back and we'd fix everything."

Mandy didn't know all the details, and Preston refused to talk about them, but she knew he'd been financially strapped for years. That's why he worked himself into the ground seven days a week. She was sure it had something to do with his family. The sad tone in his voice pulled on her heartstrings. "I appreciate it, Preston. If there's one thing I've learned in life, it's not everything can be fixed." A moth flew by her head on its way to the porch light. "I had two more calls from people wanting to buy the place. You'd think I put an ad out or something. I don't know who I can trust to purchase it and not keep it. Unless we put that in the contract. Is that possible?"

"I don't know. We can check into that." He turned his head to look at her. "Do you even know who you'd ask?"

Even as she pondered his question, she couldn't think of a single person. She had several friends, but none of them could afford such a venture. And those who might be able to, she didn't know well enough to ask for such a huge favor. Instead, she changed the subject. "What are you going to do with all the equipment in Papa's workshop?"

"I want you to come out and make sure there's nothing you want to keep, first. Then I'll see if I can find someplace to move it to. If I can get everything set up, I'd like to start my own woodworking business."

"That's great, Preston. Papa always said you had a lot of talent. Not just for working with wood, but for drawing up plans and ideas." Her voice broke. "Have you looked around? Do your parents have a space you can work out of?"

"No, there's no room at their house. I'll see how much it'll cost to rent a place for now. I'm hoping to do some calling around tomorrow."

"There's no hurry to move everything." She'd barely finished speaking when a large flying beetle zipped its way their direction. Mandy couldn't stand the obnoxious beetles and immediately ducked her head. Instead of heading to the porch light like all the other sane insects, it continued to buzz around them until it landed on her head. Mandy shuddered. "Get it off, Preston. Get it off!"

He was laughing hard as his hands went through her hair and finally dislodged the offending bug. He tossed it over the railing. With his elbows propped against the stair behind him, he leaned his head back and continued to chuckle.

"It's not funny. I hate those. The only bug in

existence that'll opt for my hair over the light like all the other ones." She stared at him as he continued to find hilarity in the event. She wanted to be annoyed, but it was impossible. His humor was contagious, and Mandy was soon laughing with him. She had to admit it felt good. "Ohhhh, I needed that. The laughter, not the bug."

"Me, too." He looked at her then, and she could scarcely make out his eyes in the semi-darkness. "I'm worried about you, Mandy."

"I'll be fine. I *am* fine." She tore her gaze from his and brushed at something invisible on her knee. "Thanks for coming back over here tonight. I know you have a million other things to do."

"Nah. Nothing that can't wait until tomorrow."

They sat in companionable silence, laughing at the antics of the families as they came in from their fun at the lake. Most of the time, Mandy was perfectly fine with her life. Yet, every once in a while, she saw happy families like these and wondered what it would be like to have her own one day. Was something like that even possible? When she spent time like this with Preston, those buried longings surfaced.

She slammed the brakes on her train of thought. What if a relationship with Preston didn't work out? What if children were involved, and they only caused them the kind of heartache she'd experienced herself? No, there were a lot of compelling reasons for why she'd sworn off marriage, and no equally convincing reasons to change her mind. She'd be better off alone.

Preston stood and offered her a hand to help her up. The moment she laid her hand in his, her blood rushed in her ears, and it felt as though his touch were branding her skin.

Mandy valued his friendship. Always had. But she couldn't let anything more develop between them. She needed the buffer, because one day, he'd find the girl for him and even he would leave. It was only a matter of time. And he deserved it—deserved to have a wife and family. Just the thought caused a pang of jealousy. Unwilling to consider the source, she remained convinced she'd be happy for him when that time came.

Regardless, the truth remained. One way or another, everyone in Mandy's life disappeared. Eventually she'd truly be alone.

Chapter Five

The rest of Preston's week was busy. He worked at the Hudson B&B until eleven and then got to Clearwater Lumber by noon. Apparently, the liquidation sale brought in nearly everyone from town because Preston didn't stop hauling materials out to vehicles until the place closed at nine in the evening. When he had a spare moment, he applied for four local job opportunities. He also called several places for rent to see how much it would cost to set up the woodworking equipment.

By Saturday morning, Preston was discouraged. All the places for rent were out of his price range. And none of that mattered, anyway, when the employment avenues weren't paying off. In one week, he'd be losing two-thirds of his income.

Mom had texted him about dinner. The thought of homemade spaghetti and garlic bread drove him to his tiny apartment to shower and change clothes before heading over to his parents' house.

Over dinner, Preston told his parents about his

part of the will. "I can't find anywhere to move the equipment to. I've called around and any place available is way too large for what I need, which also means the cost is high." He whirled spaghetti noodles around his fork and took a bite.

Dad looked thoughtful. "Does Mandy have plans for the workshop?"

"I don't know."

"Why don't you talk to her about renting it for now? The equipment's there. It'd save you some trouble and the extra money would help her, too."

Preston blinked at him. He hadn't even thought about that. Still, if she had to sell the place and something fell through, he didn't want to risk the equipment going with the B&B. He told his parents about the rest of the will and the decision Mandy faced.

Mom put her fork down on her plate and leaned forward. "I want to say I can't believe Barry and Samantha would do that. But, I can't count the times Samantha expressed concern for Mandy once Barry passed on. She worried about that poor girl being alone."

Preston tried to ignore the intense stare Dad was giving him over the rim of his coffee mug. It didn't work.

"Why don't you marry the girl? You'll have a workshop for all of your equipment and she'll keep the B&B. Sounds like a win-win to me."

"Stanley!" Mom shot her husband a stern look.

Dad shrugged, a mischievous glint in his eyes. "What? Preston's been in love with Mandy for years. This is the incentive he needs to do something about it."

Preston groaned. His reasons for wanting to tell

them in person evaporated. He should've texted instead. "I told you, Dad. Mandy's determined to not marry. Anyone. She sees me as her friend, and I doubt that'll ever change." It was a realization he'd come to after getting back from two years of college. He'd hoped distance might make Mandy's heart grow fonder. She'd expressed how much she missed him, but continued to keep him at arm's length.

It's not like he hadn't tried to move past this in his own life, but every time he thought of trying to date someone else, he knew going forward would be nearly impossible. Dad was right, Preston was head over heels in love with Mandy. It's too bad she didn't love him in return.

"So, you'll be all right standing back and watching her marry someone else if that's what she chooses to do?"

Dad was baiting him, and Preston responded immediately. "Absolutely not. If she marries someone to save her place, it'll be me." Once the words were out, his neck grew warm with the admission.

Dad gave a satisfied grunt and went back to piling spaghetti on a piece of garlic bread.

Mom didn't look convinced. "Are you talking about a marriage of convenience like they used to do? Stay married for a year making it possible for Mandy to keep the B&B and then get a divorce? I think it would be a mistake."

Well, when you put it that way... Preston sighed. "I admit it's not ideal, but it'd give me a year to prove to her we could work."

"And if you can't?"

"Then I'd have to let her go." The thought of walking away from Mandy was unfathomable.

The plate of food in front of Preston sat untouched as thoughts and ideas spun around in his head. Dad might not have a lot of tact, but he was right about one thing. The possibility of marrying Mandy had a lot of merit, and the thought of spending even more time with the woman he loved wasn't exactly a deterrent.

Convincing *her* of that, though, would be a completely different matter.

~*~

"Here, let me get that." Mandy took the fourth pan of muffins from Jade. She carefully took the muffins out and lined them up on a wire rack to cool. The combined scents of cinnamon, strawberry, and chocolate chip filled the kitchen. The pastries would be set out for their guests along with scrambled eggs, hash browns, bacon, and sausage.

No matter how Mandy made eggs, Jade's were somehow better. Even Granny commented regularly about that. It was like the woman had some special ingredient. "I'm sorry things have been so up and down here. I know it's not easy when you can't count on specific work days. Reservations were way down over the summer, and the trend just seems to be continuing." She tried to ignore the concern that made her stomach hurt.

Jade looked up from the bowl of eggs she was beating with a fork. "I understand, honey. This is more of a hobby for me. Gets me out of the house, and I enjoy cooking for others." She paused. "I admit I'm worried about you, though. Now that Mrs. Hudson is gone, I thought you might decide you'd rather not run

49

this place." The concern in her eyes was unmistakable.

"I can't leave. This is my home." Even if things weren't the same. "There are some issues with Granny's will. Combine that with the ridiculous number of people who want to purchase the property and the lack of reservations... Things aren't easy right now."

"Maybe you should think about selling." When Jade saw the shocked look on Mandy's face, she spoke quickly to clarify. "I just mean your Granny had a hard time keeping this place going over the last year. She wouldn't want you saddled with that responsibility on top of all your internet stuff."

"It's just a wrinkle, but I'll get it ironed out. No worries."

The older woman didn't look convinced, but she smiled and went back to the eggs, the metal utensil clinking against the side of the bowl. "I know you will, honey."

Mandy checked the time. "I'm meeting with Preston here in a minute. I should be back in an hour. Call me if something comes up."

"I've got it covered. You should take that young man a muffin or two."

Not a bad idea. Mandy found a paper bag and put two of each kind inside. She and Preston had agreed to talk for a while this morning and come up with a game plan for when they called the lawyer. They might as well eat breakfast at the same time.

She'd hoped to find a solution by now. She'd even talked to two of her friends about buying the B&B so she could purchase it from them again. Raven said she would if she could, but her job was still fairly new and she doubted the bank would give her a loan that large. Tricia patted her rounding belly and said they were trying to save as much money as possible before the baby was born. Both assured her they would help if they were able.

Mandy totally understood. It's wasn't something she'd be able to do, either, if they had come to her asking for the same favor.

In the end, she was right back where she'd started when she first heard about the will.

With the bag of muffins in hand, she waved to Jade and went out the back door. Preston was sitting on the steps waiting for her. He jumped to his feet and turned.

"Good morning."

Mandy smiled at him. "Good morning." She held up the bag. "I've got breakfast."

"Nice! Do you mind if we walk for a few minutes before we sit down and eat?"

"Not at all." They'd gotten a small rainstorm last night, which had cooled the air off. Since it was only six-thirty in the morning, the sun hadn't yet removed the chill. Mandy enjoyed the temporary change. The summer had been an unusually hot one, and she looked forward to the promise of cooler weather.

Preston led them across the lawn to one tree on the other side of the yard. He motioned to the ground beside it. "How does this look?"

The branches had protected the grass from what little rain they'd received and it looked dry. "Perfect."

They sat next to each other, their backs against the large tree. Mandy let him choose a muffin first then got a cinnamon one for herself. They ate in silence for a few moments before she spoke. "Did you find a place for the woodworking equipment?"

"Nope. Every place I contacted that had space for rent either wanted way too much, or the place was too small." Preston polished off the muffin and brushed the crumbs off on his pants. "That's something I wanted to talk to you about. But first, did you have any luck finding someone to purchase the B&B so you could buy it back?"

Mandy pinched a bite off her muffin and put it on her tongue, savoring the cinnamon. "I talked to someone at my bank and they said they couldn't do anything like that. I asked a couple of friends, and both of them had real reasons for saying no." She paused. "I don't want to arrange something with a stranger, but I may not have any choice. There've been a lot of people calling and offering to buy this place. I tested the water and mentioned the possibility of buying it back from them for a little more."

"And what did they say?"

She frowned. "They said they'd quadruple their money with the plans they had for the land." The thought of the B&B being torn down and the property filled with back-to-back houses made her sad. "So yeah, I'm not sure what to do. Several of the companies offered me way more money than I thought I'd get. Maybe I should take it and run." Guilt stabbed at her simply for entertaining the possibility. Granny may have said that option would be okay, but it didn't mean it was something she or Papa would've done. And if Mandy thought they'd avoid it at all costs, then that's what she planned to do, too.

Mandy turned her head to look at Preston. He was staring out toward the river, his eyes narrowed. His serious expression worried her.

"I have an idea, but you're not going to like it."

He shifted his focus to her.

Butterflies filled Mandy's stomach and her heart flip-flopped in her chest. She knew where he was going and shook her head. "No."

Preston moved until he faced her. They both sat cross legged, their knees touching. "Hear me out. And while you do, think about it logically."

She fought against the instinct to leap to her feet and walk back to the house. If she had any other options, she probably would have. Instead, she straightened her spine, set the bag of muffins on the grass beside her, and crossed her arms in front of her chest. "Go ahead."

"If we got married—" He held up a hand to stop her when she started to object. "You promised you'd hear me out." Preston waited long enough to make sure she would keep her word and continued. "If we got married, there'd be no problem with you keeping the B&B. The lawyer said you only needed to be married a year. At that point, the house and land will be yours—just as it should be. You don't have to put anything in my name."

Mandy's jaw dropped. "You're suggesting a marriage in name only? What is this, the 1800s? You're insane." She considered what he said and frowned. "So, we'd stay married for a year, and then what? Get a divorce?"

"If that's what you want." Preston's expression made it difficult for Mandy to tell what he was thinking.

Disbelief toward his idea gave way to anger. "You know what I dealt with as a kid. My parents got a divorce and signed me over to my grandparents like an old car or something. There are a lot of things I'm determined to *not* do and getting a divorce is one of them. So yeah, that's not happening."

"Then we don't get a divorce." His brows rose, and he stared at her with a look daring her to counter him. In the past, it usually preceded a list of reasons for why he was right and she was wrong.

That wouldn't work this time. He hadn't dared her to climb a tree or race him to the edge of the river. This was marriage they were talking about. And since she didn't believe in divorce, they were also talking about forever. It'd take a lot more than goading or stroking her ego to get her to agree.

She stared at him, waiting for the punch line. When he didn't break eye contact, she let her eyelids fall, blocking her view of him. She took a moment to gather her scattered thoughts. "Granny wanted this, you know." She opened her eyes again in time to see the shock on Preston's face.

"Wanted what?"

"For us to get married. She all but said that in the letter she wrote me." Mandy's mouth went dry, and she wished she'd brought something to drink along with the muffins. She cleared her throat. "I admit, if I want to keep the B&B, I don't have any other option. I'd rather sell this place than do something stupid. Or selfish."

Preston shook his head. "You're not being selfish. Or if you are, I'm just as bad. This will help me, too. I've dreamed of starting my own business, but I can't catch a break. The way things are going, I may never get the chance. Even with the equipment your grandfather gave me, I'm hard-pressed to find a place to store it or the funds to move forward with my plans." He scratched at the base of his neck and then ran his fingers through his dark blond hair. It was clear he wrestled with what he planned to say next. "I'm losing my job at Clearwater Lumber. Saturday's my last day. I have had little luck finding somewhere else to work. I don't want to, but I'll have to look outside of town if something doesn't come up soon."

Mandy blinked in shock and held up a hand to stop him. "What happened? You've worked there for years."

"Mr. Logan can't compete with the new home improvement store. He's going out of business."

She thought about all the employees who were now going to have to find somewhere else to work. "That's terrible. I'm sorry." And equally as sorry that she'd been in her own world to the point where she didn't realize this was happening.

His gray eyes settled on her and softened. "If we get married, I can help you with the B&B like I have been. I can also keep the equipment in the workshop and work toward my goals. Our goals." He paused, a small smile lifting the corners of his mouth. "So, you see, this would be helping me out, too. We can take the money I'd save by ditching the apartment and open a savings account. I'd like to get to the point where neither of us is strapped for money like this again."

Mandy didn't deny the idea held a lot of appeal. She grimaced. How could she consider this crazy deal? Her mind kept listing objection after objection, while peace flooded the rest of her body. With the mixed signals, how was she supposed to know what to do? She couldn't marry Preston, could she?

Chapter Six

Preston watched the war being waged within Mandy as different emotions played across her face. The woman was stubborn, and he knew she was going through a mental pros-and-cons list. Everything about a marriage of convenience made sense to him. It would solve both of their problems and, if things went forward with his business like he thought they would, in a few years they could be financially stable. Something he'd fought for all his life. *Come on, girl. Give us a chance.*

"We can't do this." Mandy stood, dusting off the back of her shorts.

He scrambled to his feet. "Why not?"

"I've never wanted to get married, and I'm okay with that. But you…" Her voice trailed off, and she lifted her big brown eyes to his. The sadness and uncertainty made his heart twist in his chest. "You want a family someday. You've always told me that. What if you meet the woman you want to marry while you're saddled with me? I'll sell this place to be bulldozed before I get a divorce. Where does that leave you?"

"I'm not worried about it."

"You should be."

Preston slowly shook his head as he placed his hands on her shoulders. "I'm not worried about it because I met that woman years ago." He looked up at the branches and leaves above them. "Do you recognize this tree?" It took her a moment before realization dawned. A blush climbed her neck and crept into her cheeks.

He removed one of his hands from her shoulder and gently touched beneath her chin with a finger. "I told you then I thought I'd found the girl I wanted to marry. I won't fall in love with anyone else." He let that sink in a minute. Maybe he shouldn't have overwhelmed her like that. But if they were considering this, he wanted her to know where he stood.

Mandy took a step away from him and turned toward the tree. She let her forehead rest against the bark.

Preston wished she'd say something. Anything. "I can convert part of the workshop to a room and stay out there."

The words had barely left his mouth when she rotated to face him. "No. There are plenty of rooms in the house. You're not staying in the workshop. That'd just be wrong."

"I'm not?" He couldn't contain the grin. It only spread when Mandy planted her fists on her hips as she caught onto what he'd done.

"You think you're funny, don't you?"

He got a great deal of satisfaction out of flustering her. But, if there was one thing he wanted to be clear about, it was how he felt toward her. He sobered. "No, Mandy. I'm being serious here." He reached for one of her hands. "Will you marry me?"

"I...we...we have a lot of details to go over. We need to know what we're talking about before we call the lawyer," she stammered.

It was adorable. "Mandy."

"What will we tell Jade and Elise? What about your parents?"

"Mandy!"

She stopped talking, her complete attention on him.

Preston brushed some of her silky hair away from her face and left his hand on her cheek. "Will you marry me?"

He noted the pulse in her neck quicken, and she moistened her lips with the tip of her tongue. "Yes." That one word caused relief to flood his system. Before he said anything, she lifted a hand and placed it between them. "But if you even try to kiss me, Preston, I swear..."

He tilted his head back and laughed. Now that was a challenge he was happy to accept. "Don't worry. Next time I kiss you on the mouth, it'll be because you initiate it."

"Don't hold your breath." Flustered, she retrieved the bag of muffins from the grass at her feet and tossed it at him.

He caught it easily. "You sure about this?"

"Yes." She still looked embarrassed, but that one word radiated confidence.

That was all he needed to hear. Truthfully, he had figured it'd take a lot more convincing for her to agree. "Let's sit back down and finish our breakfast. We have a lot of planning to do."

~*~

"You can still back out." Raven used a clip to secure part of Mandy's hair at the back of her head. "No one would blame you."

Tricia stood from the bed where she'd been resting her feet. "You're not helping." She pinned Raven with one of her patented friend glares before turning her attention to Mandy.

Mandy checked her reflection in the mirror. She almost didn't recognize herself in the traditional white bridal gown. In fact, she had originally intended to buy and wear a simple dress, but Tricia insisted she borrow the dress she had gotten married in since they wore the same size.

Or used to. Tricia turned sideways and stuck her baby belly out as far as it would go. "You'd never guess I could fit into that dress myself a couple of years ago." She laughed and then gave Mandy a hug. "You look beautiful, girl. I'm glad you decided to wear it. Every woman deserves to feel pretty when she gets married."

The dress flowed to her ankles and just barely covered the white slip-on shoes Mandy wore. With the exception of her grandparents' funerals, Mandy didn't wear dresses. How was it possible to feel weird, feminine, and confused all at once? She hoped Preston didn't take one look at her and think she looked silly.

Her palms were sweaty and her pulse racing. No, she wouldn't back out of this marriage, but it didn't mean she wasn't scared.

Mandy squared her shoulders. No one else had to know, though. "Thank you, Tricia. It truly is a beautiful dress." She gave her friend a hug. "I'm glad you girls could be here for this."

It was Sunday afternoon, less than a week since she and Preston had agreed to get married. It was also the first day of October. A new month, a new phase of her life. It seemed fitting, even if it was scary all at the same time. Thanks to Jade and Elise keeping an eye on the B&B, Mandy could get away for the rest of the afternoon and early evening.

Preston wanted his parents to be there for the tiny ceremony and encouraged Mandy to invite someone, too. She'd shocked Raven and Tricia when she told them about the engagement. Even though Mandy didn't get to hang out with them very often anymore, she considered them some of her closest friends. Despite their surprise, they were thrilled to be there for her, even if Raven was a little more reluctant to agree the wedding was a good idea in the first place.

Mandy was truly glad her friends were standing with her, but it didn't distract her from the knowledge it ought to be Papa and Granny. Although the fact she wouldn't be getting married in the first place if they were still alive hadn't escaped her.

She checked her watch for the tenth time in as many minutes. Preston had promised to keep it casual on his side, too. It would only be the two of them, Tricia and Raven, then Mr. and Mrs. Yarrow, and the preacher. It's not like they needed to make a big show of the event.

At least they all knew the details of this marriage. That made it a little easier. Even Pastor Dan, who had known both Preston and Mandy most of their lives, agreed their marriage and the reasons behind it had merit. Especially since neither of them were going into it with the purpose of divorce. Mandy had half expected him to laugh in their faces and suggest counseling. Instead, he'd met with them, asked questions, and given advice for how they could best start their new lives together.

Minutes later, Mandy received a text. Time to go. The three ladies exited the house and picked their way across the yard until the tree where Preston had proposed came into view. He thought it would be the perfect place for the ceremony.

Raven and Tricia walked in front of Mandy to partially block her view from the waiting groom. It blocked Mandy's view a little, too. But she could still see someone had decorated the area beneath the maple tree. Large pots of red roses lined a path to the base of the tree. There, Pastor Dan and Preston waited. Mr. and Mrs. Yarrow stood beside him. Another man Mandy didn't recognize held a camera and took photos as she approached. They'd all promised to keep the ceremony between the seven of them and Mandy would've been annoyed about the stranger if she hadn't been so nervous.

Her friends walked single file down the rose-lined aisle. The scent of roses filled the air as the hem of her gown swished around her ankles. When Raven and Tricia reached the end, and stepped to the side, Mandy got her first real look at Preston. This was the first time she'd ever seen him in a tux, and she had to admit, he cleaned up nice. The muscles he'd built up from years of woodworking and heavy lifting stretched his jacket across his shoulders. What caught her attention the most was the smile on his face and the intensity in his eyes.

And it was those gray eyes that pulled her to his

side. She couldn't miss the mixture of appreciation and something else in his expression. He leaned over to whisper in her ear.

"You look beautiful, Mandy."

Was it his words or the fact his breath fanned her ear as he spoke that sent chill bumps chasing one another across her skin? Preston took her hand in his. Suppressing a shiver, she turned to face Pastor Dan, vaguely aware of the unknown photographer who had moved to get a better view.

Pastor Dan smiled at each of them. "We are gathered here today to join this man and this woman in holy matrimony. This is a rather unusual union. But this young couple has a lot in their favor.

"Preston and Mandy have a friendship spanning more than a dozen years. They've worked side-by-side, been there for each other, and they have the support of friends and family. While I know they are entering into this marriage with one goal, I can assure you I've seen many epic loves begin with far less in their favor."

His words brought several chuckles. Preston gave her hand a gentle squeeze, and Mandy tried to ignore the heat climbing her neck. Mandy didn't miss that Pastor Dan had uttered the same words written in Granny's letter: Epic love. *I don't believe in epic loves, God. Especially not for me. But I don't want Preston or I to get hurt. Please be in this marriage and guide us. I think we're going to need it.*

Mandy focused on Pastor Dan's words and tried to steady the pounding of her heart.

"If there are no objections—" he paused for a few moments before continuing, "then let us begin." Pastor Dan gave each of them a smile.

Mandy listened as Preston repeated his vows, his

eyes never leaving hers. When it came time for her to do the same, her throat felt thick with emotions. This was something she had sworn she'd never do. Yet here she stood, pledging forever to Preston. His expression had such peace, such hope, in it. Did hers reflect the same emotions? She may not have hope that they'd actually find the "epic love" everyone kept talking about. But she did trust him, and that's what she drew on as she spoke her vows.

They exchanged the simple wedding bands they'd chosen the other day. Preston had promised he'd buy her something prettier, but she assured him she preferred the shiny band.

As he slid the warm metal onto her finger, everything they promised each other became exceedingly real.

"With the power vested in me by the state of Texas and our almighty God, I now pronounce you husband and wife."

To Mandy's relief, Pastor Dan didn't include, "You may kiss the bride," and the clapping from around them buffered the missing sentiment. Preston surprised her by lifting her hand and dropping a light kiss to her knuckles. When he looked into her eyes, the combination of kindness and something else she didn't recognize, sent Mandy's heart into a series of cartwheels.

He released her hand as hugs were exchanged all around. Mrs. Yarrow embraced Mandy with a tearful, "Welcome to the family, sweetheart."

Family.

Tears threatened and Mandy's throat constricted as all the implications of that word crashed into her at once. She had a new family. According to God and the law of men, Preston was now her family. And her grandparents, the only family she'd had until now, were gone. They should've been here for this. Were they smiling down from heaven right now? Were they happy with her decision?

Preston's laugh snagged her attention. He seemed at ease visiting with everyone. When he caught her gaze, he offered her one of the sweetest smiles she had ever seen. The realization of what he'd given up for her hit Mandy like a brick. He'd promised her forever, even though he knew it would be a marriage without affection or intimacy. Why would he agree to something like that? It sounded crazy, even to her. Unless he hoped things would change—that she'd change.

What had she done? The weight of her emotions pressed down on her until drawing a breath was almost more than she could bear.

~*~

Preston was visiting with Pastor Dan when he saw Mandy standing alone near the tree. No one else seemed to notice the small change in his new bride's demeanor, but Preston was on immediate alert. He was about to go to her when Mom intercepted. "The photographer was wondering if the two of you would like a picture together."

When Mom had said they wanted to pay for a photographer, Preston objected. But she assured him that one day, their marriage would be more than it was now, and that Mandy would be glad she had photos to remember it by. Preston had agreed, but had not found the chance to talk to Mandy about it himself.

"Let me ask her."

He stepped beside Mandy and put an arm around her waist. "Hey, you okay?" Her lashes lifted, and the grief in her eyes mixed with something else he couldn't identify. The combination caused him to tighten his hold on her. "Your grandparents?" She nodded. "I miss them, too. They should be here. They'd want to be here. I know they are watching over you right now." *God, please ease Mandy's grief, even just a little. Fill her with the peace only You can grant. Help me to know what I can do to make things easier for her.*

Mandy took a steadying breath and gave another little nod. She turned her head toward the others.

Preston let go of her but reached for her hand. "Don't worry about everyone else. They all understand how hard this must be for you." He hesitated. What he wanted to do was get her back to the house where she could have a few minutes to breathe. He knew she wouldn't leave yet, though. Not with his family and her friends still there. "My mom wondered if you'd like the photographer to take a few pictures of us and the wedding party before he leaves. If you'd rather not, we'll all understand."

"It's okay. That'll be fine." Mandy used her hands to smooth her hair and brush invisible wrinkles out of her dress. "It was kind of your mom to hire him," she responded, although her expression belied her words. She looked down at her bridal gown. "Besides, this may be the last time I ever wear a dress. You know what they say: It didn't happen without pictures to prove it."

He chuckled. "You look beautiful no matter what you wear. But for the record? You make that dress look good."

Mandy ducked her head, a smile on her face. "Thank you. It was nice of Tricia to let me borrow it."

"We'll take a few pictures, all go back to the house to eat some of Jade's cake, and then hopefully things will quiet down."

"That'll be good."

He held an arm out for her. "You going to be okay?"

She slipped her hand into the crook of his arm and lifted her chin. "Of course." And with that, Mandy's usual determination was firmly in place again.

Preston didn't understand how she maintained the emotional control she exhibited so often. Everyone had their limits, and poor Mandy would reach hers, eventually. He only hoped he could be there to help her and support her when she did.

Chapter Seven

A mini celebration followed the wedding ceremony, and then Raven, Tricia, and Pastor Dan left. Mr. and Mrs. Yarrow helped Preston bring some of his belongings from his apartment over to the B&B.

Mandy stood in the doorway of what used to be Papa's study. It was a spacious room with a large walk-in closet and a big window looking out over the front yard. It also happened to be the room across from her own. Granny's was a little larger and one door down from hers, but Mandy hadn't had the courage to clean it out yet, and Preston insisted he didn't mind.

These three rooms were upstairs on one side of the house while the three rooms they normally rented out were on the other. There was a large bathroom on both sides as well, plus a private one attached to Granny's room.

Preston had walked his parents out to their car. She heard his footsteps coming down the hall and stop. "You sure you don't mind me taking this room?" His deep voice came from right behind her.

He'd asked the question three times now. Mandy hated there was something in the way she acted that prompted him to continue seeking confirmation of her decision.

"I'm sure. It's crazy how much can change in a year, isn't it?" She didn't expect an answer. She surveyed his room with the bed, dresser, and small stack of boxes. "Is this all you have? You can store anything else in the workshop if it won't fit in here." She turned to look at him.

"There's nothing else. I sold everything I didn't have space for. This place has all the furniture it needs, which meant the couch and dining room table had to go. I don't mind. It'll give us a little extra money to work with when it comes to opening the woodworking business."

His use of the word "us" made Mandy frown and warmed her all at the same time. He already considered them to be one unit. She hoped he wouldn't regret the whole thing in a year or two when their arrangement was still exactly like it was now.

They might be married. She may be Mrs. Mandy Yarrow. That didn't mean she was willing to surrender her heart, especially knowing firsthand how easily the fragile organ could be crushed into a million pieces.

Preston would have to be content with being partners when it came to their last name and the businesses. She intended to keep everything else firmly in the friend zone.

He pointed down the hall. "Are any guests staying tonight?"

"Yes, all three rooms are rented out, can you believe it? One is a wildlife photographer who said she'll only be in to sleep and for breakfast. The other is a family of four. The kids are staying in one room and the parents in the other." She glanced at her watch. "I think they went into town to see a movie at the old theater tonight."

He seemed unsure. "I have to admit, this will take some getting used to. I've been living in my apartment on my own for a while, so all the people going in and out of here will be interesting."

Since Granny died, Mandy had been eating all meals except for breakfast on her own in the kitchen. Having someone else to eat with had a lot of appeal. "If it helps, it'll take some adjusting on my part, too. I tend to eat lunch and dinner when I feel like it…"

"I'll follow your lead. I don't want to be in the way." He leaned against the opposite doorframe not far from Mandy. "I figure I'll use next week to take inventory of the equipment in the workshop and draw up a business plan. While I'd love to jump in and build something, I want to do this right." He paused, as though searching for the words to say. "I don't want to step on any toes. If there's anything I can help with here in the B&B, please let me know."

His offer seemed genuine, and Mandy gave him a little smile. "Sounds like a plan. Likewise, with the workshop. If I can do anything, please tell me. I'm not familiar with the equipment, other than watching Papa sometimes."

They regarded each other for several moments before Mandy lowered her gaze and backed away from the room. "I'll leave you to get settled. Your mom brought a casserole and salad over for dinner tonight. I figured we could have that if it sounds good."

"Sure."

"About six?"

"That works."

She gave him a little wave and headed back downstairs. *Well, that wasn't awkward at all.*

Mandy looked for something to do to keep her mind occupied, but Jade and Elise had not only done their jobs, they'd made certain everything else was good to go. That left Mandy with nothing to do but wipe clean counters or straighten up the living room in case some of the guests came through. Truthfully, it would've been easier if the place had been left a mess. Mandy would rather be furiously cleaning. It was moments like these, when the quiet crept in, that she hated being alone. Except she wasn't completely alone, was she? She was married now, and had no idea what to expect. Would things change, or would they pretty much remain the same? She wasn't sure which one would be easier.

Preston had spent a great deal of time at the Hudson Bed & Breakfast growing up it was practically a second home to him. But working outside, having cookies in the kitchen, and helping Mr. Hudson in the workshop was one thing.

It was different to walk upstairs to a bedroom that was now his when he never would've dared to step foot on the second level of the home before. He kept thinking Mrs. Hudson would ask him what he was doing and suggest he go back downstairs again.

Couple that with the idea he might run into guests on his way up or down added another level of weird. Obviously, people got used to it. Mr. and Mrs. Hudson, along with Mandy, lived most of their lives with strangers in their midst. But right now, Preston felt like he ought to tiptoe to keep from disturbing anyone.

He chuckled despite himself. Hopefully, he'd feel more at home before too long.

Preston changed shirts, washed up, and headed downstairs. The smell of Mom's beef and cheese enchiladas filled the air. He found Mandy in the kitchen, reaching above her head for some plates in one cabinet.

"Here, let me." Preston grabbed two of the plates, their smooth surfaces cool to the touch. "These cabinets are surprisingly high."

Mandy motioned to a foot stool on the other side of the room. "Granny had to use that for almost everything. She never complained, though." A wistful smile teased her lips. "I don't have to use it nearly as often. But you…" She looked at him. "Well, you have no problem reaching much of anything, do you?"

What did she think of his height? Growing up, it'd often come in handy for getting things she couldn't quite reach. Then again, she'd also been frustrated when they'd race to see who climbed a tree first. Every time he won, she'd claim it was because he cheated, being so tall and all. He smiled at the memory. "Where do you want me to put these?"

She hesitated. "I've been eating in here, but we can go to the dining room if you'd prefer."

"Nope, this is good." He set the plates down in front of the two chairs arranged side-by-side at the bar in the middle of the kitchen. "You know, this is where I sat when your grandmother gave me cookies or muffins. I always thought it was sweet of her to share like she did."

"Yeah. That was Granny." Mandy turned away from him before he could see her face.

He hoped she was doing okay and having him there wasn't making things harder. That was the last thing he wanted. "Is there anything else I can get for you?"

"We should be good." By the time she returned with the salad and forks, her expression was firmly in neutral.

"Do you want me to pray?" A single nod said she did, and he said a prayer over their food. The next few moments were spent in general conversation as they filled their plates.

Mandy pointed to her enchiladas with her fork. "These are great. I'll have to remember to tell your mom."

"She can make some mean Mexican food." Preston took a bite of salad and washed it down with a drink of ice water.

More silence.

Preston cringed. "This is weird."

Mandy slumped with a sigh of relief. "Really weird."

They both laughed a little.

Preston put his fork down. "Look, Mandy. I'm your friend. A ring on your finger, no matter what brought it around, doesn't change that fact. It never will." He held his arms out wide. "Think of me as the live-in fix-it guy. I can take care of the B&B's landscape like normal, and I'm here in case of an emergency repair 24/7. No having to wait until the next day."

"That's true. Hopefully, this will be easier on you. No more working two jobs in different locations. I still don't know how you managed that."

"You do what you have to do." He shrugged as she nodded. That was one trait they both had in common. No matter what life threw at them, they did what needed to be done. The fact they sat here, married, was evidence of that. Maybe now that they were working together, some of that wouldn't be as hard. "It's a relief to not have to haul wood twenty times a day. Or eat by myself every evening."

A little smile tugged at her lips. "Not eating by myself would be nice. And on the nights we don't have guests, I won't freak out sleeping in this house alone. I swear this place feels haunted by a million ghosts when no one else is here."

They looked at each other for a few moments, and Preston wished he knew what was going through her pretty head. Her posture suggested she was relaxing, but her eyes still looked guarded. Preston finally spoke. "Then you can add 'ghost slayer' to the list of my duties."

That got a little chuckle out of her. "Works for me."

"Friends, then?"

"Friends."

"Good." He leaned over and bumped her shoulder with his and then chortled when she struggled to not fall out of her chair.

The sparkle in her eyes mixed with determination, which was more like the normal Mandy he was used to seeing. He winked at her, and they both continued their meal.

A few moments later, her phone rang. Mandy fished it out of her pocket and scowled a little as she hit the button to answer the call. "Hudson Bed & Breakfast. How can I help you?"

Preston could barely make out the low tenor of the caller, and none of the words spoken. Mandy opened her mouth two or three times to respond, but it was clear she wasn't given a chance to get a word in edgewise. A look of annoyance passed over her face, and she finally broke into the one-sided conversation.

"I'm sorry, but your source of information was incorrect. The B&B is not for sale." Another round of talking on the other end of the call began. This time, Mandy cut him off in seconds. "The offer makes no difference. I'm not selling this place. Please make a note so other people in your company don't call me as well." With that, she hung up. She shoved the offending phone back into her pocket and stared wearily at the food on her plate.

"People are still trying to buy this place?"

"I'm getting several calls a day. Two companies called multiple times as though harassing me will change my mind." She jabbed her fork into the enchilada but then left it there. "Does this happen to everyone who loses a family member and has a business? There ought to be laws in place to prevent this kind of thing." Her annoyance faded to sadness as she scooped a bite into her mouth.

"I had no idea they were bothering you like that. Next time any of those companies call back, hand the phone to me. I'll make sure they don't call you again."

Her eyes met his with uncertainty. She thought about it a moment before agreeing. "Thank you."

"You're welcome. The dust will settle, Mandy. I promise."

Preston knew there would be rough days ahead as she mourned the loss of her family. He hoped his presence somehow made it all a little better. He watched her for a moment and embraced the surge of protectiveness washing over him. The woman he had loved for much of his life needed him, whether she'd admit it or not. *Show me how I can help, God. Mandy's been through so much. Help her come out on the other side of this even stronger than before. Make our relationship stronger, too.*

Chapter Eight

Growing up, Mandy usually awoke early each day and, without fail, she'd find Granny already in the kitchen. That's when they would chat about the day and often bake together. Since Granny died, Mandy found she had to set her alarm to remind herself to get up early. She had no real desire to enter an empty kitchen and preferred to make it down there minutes before Jade showed up for the morning.

The morning after the wedding, however, Mandy's eyes flew open. She had known it was early since there wasn't a hint of sunrise coming through the window. At first, she lay in her bed, listening for sounds of life in the house, but she heard nothing but the birds singing outside.

When an attempt to go back to sleep failed, Mandy got out of bed with a sigh. She might as well get the day started. She'd opted for a shower in Granny's bathroom instead of the one she shared with Preston. She rationalized it by thinking she wouldn't be taking up the usual bathroom in case he needed it when he got up. Come to think of it, she didn't know what time he normally woke up. As she soaped her hair with shampoo, Mandy admitted she didn't want to run into Preston coming out of the bathroom. Not yet. Maybe she couldn't hide forever, but seeing as this was their first full day as a married couple in a less-than-typical marriage, surely no one would blame her for doing so right now.

By the time she ran a comb through her wet hair and French braided it down her back, a hazy light appeared on the eastern horizon. She dressed quickly and stepped out into the hallway. Preston's bedroom door was open a crack, but the light off. Had he already left? She caught a whiff of the scent that always reminded her of him. Was it his aftershave? Mandy didn't know, but the woodsy smell mixed with a touch of allspice was all Preston.

The guests didn't seem to be up yet. Mandy quietly made her way downstairs to the kitchen, half expecting to see Preston waiting. The light was on, but the room stood empty. A small note waited on the fridge.

Mandy,

I'm out at the workshop taking inventory. I'll come grab something for breakfast here in a while, and I'll start work on the B&B list before lunch. Call me if you need anything.

Preston

Knowing she wouldn't have to worry about running into him for a while set off a strange mix of relief and disappointment. Mandy pushed that aside as

Jade walked up to the back door.

"Good morning, Mandy. It looks like it'll be a lovely day today."

"Hi, Jade. I haven't been outside yet. I thought it was supposed to be hot."

Jade set down the paper bag she carried and patted at her graying hair to make sure the bun was still secure. "That's why the early morning hours are my favorite." She flashed Mandy one of her brilliant smiles. "I hope the guests are ready for crepes today."

Mandy's stomach growled on cue. Jade made the best crepes in Clearwater and they were no secret.

Jade laughed. "I'll take that as a yes." She sobered a moment. "Did you want to make the muffins, or would you like me to?"

The crepes were so sweet, Granny often made a batch of banana nut muffins and another of cinnamon muffins to give the guests an alternate choice. Mandy fought against the waves of pain radiating through her chest. She couldn't hide from reality forever. "I'll make them."

The older woman stepped forward and gave Mandy a tight hug. "Everything will be okay."

That's what Mandy kept telling herself about every five minutes.

They worked in comfortable silence for a half hour before Mandy's phone rang. She saw the area code, glared at the screen, and ignored it.

Jade flipped a crepe on the hot pan and looked up. "You don't look happy."

"I'm sure it's someone else wanting to buy the B&B." Mandy noticed how quiet Jade was. "What's wrong?"

"I worry about you running this place by

yourself, Mandy. You've got a husband now. You need to rely on each other." Jade looked concerned as she placed the finished crepe on a plate and poured batter on the hot skillet to make the next one.

Mandy's thoughts flew to Preston. If his business took off like she thought it would, he'd be doing less around the B&B before long. Mandy had to approach this from the standpoint of managing it herself and proceed from there. The last thing she wanted to do was rely on Preston more than she should.

Jade shot her a funny look. Mandy tried to give her a reassuring smile. "It'll take some adjustment, but everything will be fine."

"I know it will be." Jade gave her a wink and went back to making her crepes.

Mandy slid two pans of muffins into the oven and remembered something. "Oh! I have to get something out in the mail. I'll be right back." She hurried into the dining room and picked up the stack of thank-you notes addressed to all the people who'd brought by food or flowers for the funeral. She just hadn't had the energy to write them last week.

The wildlife photographer sat in the living area, flipping through a book. No doubt she'd been enticed to come out of hiding by the delicious smells of the promised breakfast.

Mandy opened the front door and noticed the warm air as it rushed inside. She was so ready for the weather to realize it was October and cool down a little more.

With one hand on the railing, she paused when she spotted Preston coming toward the house from the driveway. He looked up and noticed her, too, waving with a smile.

She smiled and returned the wave, then proceeded down the steps to the driveway. On the third step from the bottom, the wood gave way with a crack. Her foot twisted and slipped through the opening, sending her backward into the other steps as envelopes flew everywhere.

~*~

Preston sprinted toward the house. "Mandy! Are you okay?"

She held a hand to her lower back, and her face twisted in pain. When Preston reached for his phone, she shook her head and held up the other hand, telling him to wait.

He reached down and put a hand on her arm. "Take your time."

Mandy still sat on the step she'd fallen back on. "I'm all right." She touched her back on the right side and winced. She tugged her dark purple T-shirt up a little to reveal a long, thin bruise forming where she'd landed against the edge of a step.

Preston touched her skin lightly. "You didn't crack a rib, did you?"

She jerked the shirt back down. Preston wondered if she'd noticed the same zing of electricity from the contact he had, or if she was being extra modest.

"No, just a bruise, but I don't think I can get my foot out."

He grabbed hold of her shoe and gently twisted it to get it back through the broken step. "I can't believe this happened. Praise God you weren't hurt worse."

Mandy stood to her feet and tested her ankle. "No kidding." She groaned. "Can you imagine if this had happened to one of the guests instead? I'm glad it was me." She gave a little hop. "Yeah, my ankle's fine."

They both leaned down at the same time to retrieve the nearest envelope on the ground. Their fingers touched. Mandy lifted her head, and only then did Preston appreciate how closely they stood.

Here they were on day one of their highly unconventional marriage, and Preston had to fight every instinct in his body not to kiss his new bride. If Mandy could read his thoughts, she'd probably deck him. Or at least try. He stifled a grin.

When all the envelopes were gathered, he offered to take them to the mailbox for her. "Then I'll get some wood and repair the step before I come in for breakfast. We don't want anyone else falling on their way down. Save me something, will you?"

"I will." Her face looked a little flushed and Preston wished he knew if it was from the accident, the warm air, or something else entirely. "Thanks, Preston. Come on in whenever you're ready."

"Will do." He watched her pick her way up the stairs and disappear inside.

There were many good things about having a workshop on site, one of them being no shortage of wood. It didn't take long to locate a board he could use. Armed with that, a saw, a hammer, and some nails, he set out to pry up the broken step.

Once he had it loose, Preston sized and hammered in the replacement board. The other steps seemed to be fine, although he'd need to sand and re-stain the porch again soon. He added that to his mental to-do list.

After storing his tools in the workshop, he went inside the B&B and inhaled deeply as the scents of various baked goods pummeled his senses.

The dining room was busy as the family of four chatted over plates filled with crepes and muffins. The large table along one wall held platters of food. Preston's stomach let loose a growl in response.

Mandy came into the room, a carafe of orange juice in her hands. She placed it on the long table and picked the nearly empty one up. She motioned for him to follow her back into the kitchen. Jade stood at the sink washing dishes.

Mandy pulled a covered plate from the oven. "I put three crepes aside and some muffins. I know you like blueberry best, but I saved some with the strawberry topping, too."

He grinned at her and took one chair at the bar. "Perfect. Thank you."

She returned his smile with a brilliant one of her own. "You're welcome." She put the old carafe in the sink.

"Have you eaten yet?"

"No, but I usually don't until the guests are gone and I've cleaned up." She walked past him again.

He reached out and snagged her arm with his hand. "You should have something while it's still warm."

Jade turned from her spot in front of the sink. "I've been telling her that every morning, and she won't listen to me." She hiked an eyebrow as though daring Preston to do something about it.

He took in the stubborn look on Mandy's face and tilted his head toward the chair next to his. "Come eat with me." His hand still touched her arm, and that's where her gaze landed.

Jade gave Mandy a pointed stare. "I've got these. Sit and eat with your new husband." When she turned away, she had a grin on her face.

Mandy's cheeks turned pink as she stalked into the dining room. She returned with a plate containing a crepe and a cinnamon muffin. When she sat down, she was careful to keep her gaze on the food.

They ate in near silence. Preston wasted no time in putting away his breakfast.

"Everything was excellent." He popped the last bite of muffin in his mouth. "I may not eat again for a week."

Jade looked pleased. "I'm glad you liked it. The crepes are a family recipe. Mandy here made the muffins."

"They were great."

Mandy's little smile didn't quite reach her eyes. "Thank you."

Concern welled up in Preston. He wanted to ask her if she was okay, but her expression begged him to let it go.

"I guess I'd better get back to work. What time are you eating lunch, Mandy?"

Her eyes widened. "Usually around noon."

"I'll be in then. Holler if you need anything."

"I will."

Preston took his leave, even though he would much rather stay and spend the morning with his new wife. He suspected she needed a little space.

Chapter Nine

The moment Mandy exited the lawyer's office on Friday, she released a deep sigh of relief. She knew there shouldn't have been any hiccups, but she'd still dreaded the visit. Everything had gone planned. Preston had the contents of the workshop signed over to him. Mandy currently had control of the B&B and surrounding land and would receive the title a year from the date of their marriage.

They got settled in Preston's Dodge and looked at each other.

"Well, we did it," he said, a smile on his face. "We won't have to walk back into that office for almost a year."

"Thank goodness. Lawyers give me hives." It felt good to joke. She'd rather have the title to the B&B in her hands, but this was as close as she'd get for now.

Preston motioned to the clock on the dash. "We still have an hour before Jade expected us back. Can I take you out to lunch?"

Mandy hesitated. She should probably get home

since being away from the B&B meant Jade or Elise having to keep an eye on things. She didn't like turning control over to anyone else, even if she trusted both ladies.

"You can't do it all by yourself. I'm hoping, once we get financially stable, we can hire someone who can stay full-time during the day to help you." Before she could object, he held up a hand and continued. "Not that you can't handle all of this. But you shouldn't have to, especially when you're trying to juggle all your web clients, too. Come on, let me buy you lunch. My treat." He winked.

Mandy's resolve melted. "Fine, lunch would be great."

He grinned as though he'd won some kind of challenge against her, and Mandy let it go with a shake of her head.

Nearly a half-hour later, they sat at one of the local Mexican restaurants, a steaming platter of chicken fajitas between them. Mandy scooped some of the mixture onto a warm flour tortilla, topped it with cheese and sour cream, and took a bite. "Oh my gosh, this is incredible." She closed her eyes and nodded appreciatively.

When she opened them again, she found Preston watching her, a crooked smile on his face. The interest in his eyes made her cheeks warm, and she quickly set the fajita down and picked up her phone, hoping someone had sent her an e-mail to distract her. Maybe he didn't see her reaction. Yeah, right.

Preston tapped her foot with his underneath the table. When she raised her gaze to his, he gave her a little wink. "Remind me to take you out for fajitas more often."

"Shut up." Mandy balled up a napkin and tossed it at him. He laughed hard then, defusing the embarrassing situation. "You always know what to say, don't you?"

"It's a gift."

The man could be aggravating. Yet sitting here with him now reminded Mandy of the many days they spent together as kids. Mandy's life had rarely been worry-free, but she'd been able to ignore the difficulties when she was around Preston.

He'd had so many dreams for his future back then. Hopefully he'd get the chance to realize some of them now. "Can I ask you a question?"

"Always." When Preston noticed the serious look on her face, his brows came together and he set his drink down. "What is it?"

"You had all those plans when we were kids. You even went to college to work toward them. What happened? I mean, I know it had to do with money. You never really talked about it."

He leaned against the back of the booth, his eyes on the ceiling fan whirling not far from them. The breeze it created was just strong enough to blow the edges of his napkin back and forth. Mandy wondered if he would refuse to tell her when he finally spoke.

"You're aware of when my dad got sick and had to have the kidney transplant?"

She nodded.

"The medical bills piled up so high, my parents couldn't see their way through them. The costs of the hospital stay, the transplant itself, not to mention all the treatment leading up to the surgery..." He shrugged. "They'll probably be paying those bills until their last breath. They refused to let me help them.

Before they released my dad from the hospital, I volunteered to pick up his anti-rejection meds from the pharmacy. When I got there, I found out it was way out of their price range, and that was going to be every time they had the medication filled." He told her the cost and she gasped. "My parents couldn't afford that." He swallowed hard.

Mandy knew he'd stepped in and done something to help. That's who Preston was.

"I paid for the medication and spoke with the pharmacist. I told him about the situation and he set it up for me to pay for the medication from now on, only charging my parents a twenty-dollar copay." Preston folded his hands and placed them behind his head. "That's what I've been doing ever since. It may mean holding two jobs for the rest of my life, but if that's what it takes to keep them in their house and not going completely bankrupt, then that's what I'll do."

Mandy's heart climbed into her throat. She'd had no idea he put that kind of money out to help his parents all this time. No wonder he'd worked tirelessly for as long as she'd known him. He'd had to.

Preston must've taken her silence and pensive expression to mean she was upset. He lowered his hands to the table and leaned forward. "I'm sorry. I probably should've talked to you before we got married. But I can't stop helping them. I'll get an evening job if that's what's needed. I'm praying this new business venture will be the answer. For all of us."

The vulnerability in his eyes and the worry on his face struck Mandy right in the heart. Without thinking, she reached across the table and put her hand on top of his. "You're a good son, Preston. Of course you should continue to help them. They're lucky to have you."

He looked down at their hands and shifted his own to cradle hers. "I want you to know I will take care of you, too. Of us. I promise."

"I know." There were a lot of things in life she was uncertain of, but she knew without a doubt he spoke the truth.

He placed a kiss on the top of her hand before releasing it.

Mandy resisted the urge to touch the skin he'd just kissed. Instead, she picked up her glass and cupped it with both hands. "How are things looking in the workshop?"

"There are more materials than I thought, which is great. I have a lot of things I want to build. I'm looking forward to it." He grinned. "Oh! Your grandfather had a canoe he built in the back. I found another one that he never got the chance to complete. I'm hoping we can finish it for him." He cleared his throat. "Anyway, if all goes well, I hope I can start building on Monday."

Mandy couldn't get over how excited he was. "That's awesome! I'm happy it's all coming together."

"Me, too." He took a drink of his soda. "We still have a way to go, but at least it all seems feasible. We'll probably need a website for the business. I've had some ideas for a while. Maybe I can show them to you at dinner in the next couple of days?"

"That sounds great."

He rewarded her with another big grin. As they continued to eat, Mandy marveled at what a great team they made. They'd only been married four days, and she was getting used to his company. Considering how determined she was not to give her heart over to any man, this level of comfort probably wasn't a good thing. Preston said something that made her laugh, and she pushed her ponderings to the back of her mind.

~*~

Preston shifted his cell phone from one hand to the other as he locked the workshop behind him a week later. "I'm glad Dad seems to be better now."

"Me, too. He knew he needed to rest but was still going crazy." His dad spoke in the background and Mom laughed. "Yes, and taking me along with him."

Preston smiled. "I'm glad you both survived." He'd called his parents to talk to them for a while and to see how his dad was doing. They'd all thought about getting together last weekend, but Dad ended up with a minor cold. Not a big deal normally, but ever since the kidney transplant, it made Preston nervous anytime Dad didn't feel well.

"We'd love for you and Mandy to come over for dinner next week."

"Let me talk to her and see what kind of guest schedule we have. That'd be great, though. Can I get back to you tomorrow with a date?" Preston walked towards the house. He hadn't been by to see them since he and Mandy had gotten married almost two weeks ago. He felt bad for the lack of visits, but his parents both assured him it was good he was spending time at the B&B and with Mandy.

"Of course. We're thinking about you both."

"Thanks, Mom. I'm looking forward to seeing you. I'll talk to you soon. Love you."

"We love you, too."

They said their goodbyes and Preston hung up.

He and Mandy had gotten into a routine where they ate dinner together almost every night. He went in through the back door but there was no sign of Mandy in the kitchen, dining room, or living room. Concerned, he headed upstairs and found her sitting on the floor of her bedroom with her laptop. If the scowl on her face was any indication, things weren't going well.

She must have heard him approach because she looked up in surprise. "Hey! Oh no. What time is it?" She glanced at the clock on her laptop and stood. "I'm sorry. I completely lost track of the time. I'll bet you're starving."

Preston walked into the room. "I'm sure you are, too." He took in the blues and yellows decorating the room and thought it perfectly matched Mandy's personality. He motioned to the computer. "What's going on?"

Mandy sighed as she sank onto the end of the bed, the laptop balanced on her lap. "I'd been dreading it, but I finally went through the books Granny kept." She closed the laptop and put it down, retrieved a notebook, and rejoined Preston. "I'm amazed she and Papa kept this place running as long as they have. I knew things were tight but had no idea it was this bad."

Preston took the notebook and scanned it. She wasn't exaggerating. The financial outlook for the B&B looked grim. He sat down on the bed. "Were they relying on funds from summer to carry them through the rest of the year?"

"Except for a couple of holidays, it sure looks like it. We didn't have nearly the business this last summer that we usually do. Granny's heart just wasn't in it. We've had one cancellation, and there are only two reservations in the books for the next month and a half and both are next week. That's pathetic, even for this time of the year."

He hated the tone of dejection in her voice. "I'm sorry, Mandy. I had an idea. I don't know if it'll help, but it's worth a shot."

"Oh?" She took the notebook and tossed it onto the small desk against one wall. "I'm all ears."

Preston angled his body to face her more. "You remember those boats I told you I found in the workshop?" She nodded. "I was thinking we could finish the other one and include boat rentals with the stay here at the B&B. Make sure we have life jackets on hand, have guests sign waivers, and they could rent a boat for an hour. We don't even have to charge for it. The boats might bring in more business if we advertise it." He paused, trying to gauge Mandy's reaction. She was deep in thought. "What do you think?"

"That's a great idea. We can take some pictures and add them to the website. I want to finish the website for your business, too. We can even link to that, show that the boats they can rent were handmade and each one of a kind. It might make a good segue into what you craft. Maybe it'll drum up some sales for you, too." The weariness fled her eyes as she seemed to sift through ideas in her head. "Did you decide on a name for the business?"

He was glad she liked his suggestion. And the idea of tying it to the new business was a good one. Truthfully, Preston wasn't sure any of this was going to help the B&B in the long run, but the defeated look on Mandy's face had disappeared. That was good enough for now. "I was thinking of calling it Yarrow Woodworking."

She smiled. "I like it."

They took her laptop downstairs and ate sandwiches while they went over some last-minute website details and chatted about Yarrow Woodworking. Preston hoped there'd be a day when she considered it *their* business instead of only his.

He had an idea, though. If everything went according to plan, he hoped to get Mandy away from the B&B and remind her what it was like to relax and enjoy life. He just had to wait until Sunday morning to put it all into play.

Chapter Ten

"I shouldn't leave. What if someone drives in and wants to rent a room?"

Preston handed Mandy's phone to her. "Then we put a sign saying to call you and that someone will be back as soon as possible. How many walk-ins do you usually get?"

"Maybe one a month. Sometimes fewer." And never on a Sunday. Mandy knew she was losing this battle. Preston surprised her this morning when he'd suggested they go to church together for the first time since they'd been married. After that, he wanted to take a picnic and try out a canoe, paddling it down river before stopping to eat lunch. The adventure of it all sounded wonderful, but Mandy's practical side insisted she should stay at the house. And it wasn't only because someone might stop by. It'd been two weeks since the wedding, and Mandy could tell she was softening toward Preston. The whole prospect was scary. How could fourteen days with Preston threaten twenty-six years of swearing away marriage?

But the look on Preston's face told her he wasn't about to back down. She could stay at the house, alone, missing Granny and Papa, or she could go with Preston for the day. Her heart was in danger either way. In the end, the hope in his eyes as he kept his gaze on her face made it impossible to say no.

"Fine."

"Yes!" He grinned and pumped a fist, bringing a smile to Mandy's face as she shook her head at him. "Okay, church is in about an hour. Meet you down here in forty-five minutes?"

"I'll be here."

Once ready, they grabbed some muffins left over from the day before and headed into town.

Mandy had to admit she'd been dreading going back to church since Granny's funeral. All she could picture was the service and the overwhelming attention of the congregation during one of the most difficult moments of her life. She expected those emotions to come back, but as Preston pulled his truck into a parking spot, nothing but peace flooded her spirit. *Sorry, God, I should've come back before now.*

Preston came around to open her door. Their hands found each other's in such a natural way, Mandy wasn't sure who had initiated the contact. They entered the sanctuary together.

Mr. and Mrs. Yarrow spotted them and waved from a row toward the middle. Preston and Mandy waved back, but he moved to steer her in a different direction.

Mandy leaned closer so she could talk over the music playing in the air. "We can sit with them if you'd like. I don't mind."

His eyebrows lifted. "You're sure?"

"Of course."

A pleased look crossed his face, and he offered her a smile that reinforced her decision. Mrs. Yarrow gave her a warm hug and Mr. Yarrow offered a nod of approval. Mandy listened as the three chatted about the last week. She knew that Preston had usually had dinner at their house once a week before they got married. As far as she knew, he hadn't since. Did he feel obligated to stay around the B&B now? Family was important, and she didn't like the thought he might not be seeing his family for fear of offending her.

She was still thinking on the subject when worship began. After the message and a final prayer, the congregation stood to gather their things. Mrs. Yarrow turned toward Preston and Mandy. "We've got a roast and potatoes in the slow cooker if you two would like to join us for dinner tonight. We know the offer is last-minute. If you have other plans, we certainly understand."

Preston hesitated and the thoughts Mandy had been parsing through earlier came back. She wanted him to know he could spend time with his family. "I don't think we have any plans for tonight, do we?"

He studied her face as though trying to figure something out. "No, we don't." Then he mouthed, "Are you sure?" She gave a subtle nod. He smiled and turned back to his parents. "That sounds great."

They finalized the plans before heading back to the parking lot. He flinched as the warm air met them at the door. It was October, and Preston was more than ready for some cooler weather soon.

He reached for Mandy's hand and gave it a gentle squeeze. "Thank you for everything you did in there."

"You're welcome."

Half an hour later, they'd picked up sandwiches from Mandy's favorite deli and were back at the house. After changing and then packing a cooler with the sandwiches, chips, and drinks, they headed back outside.

Preston took the cooler from her. "I've got the canoe and everything else we need out at the dock." He led the way. Dressed in cargo shorts and a navy-blue T-shirt, he looked like he was ready for almost anything. Mandy had to hurry to keep up with his long strides as they crossed the grass to the dock.

As they approached, the sun bounced off the golden hues of the canoe Papa had built. Mandy always admired the beauty of the cedar strips used to craft it. She'd gone on several maiden voyages with her grandfather to test different boats, and she could still see the pride in his eyes as the vessel had sailed just as he intended. "Papa would like your idea of offering canoe rentals to the guests."

Preston turned his head to look at her. His eyes looked sad, but the corners of his mouth lifted. "I hope so. He did such beautiful work, and it took years for him to gather the materials for each one. It'd be nice if people enjoyed these instead of having them sit in the workshop." He paused when they reached the docks, and Mandy wished she knew what he was thinking.

He'd worked with Papa all the time. She imagined this trip probably brought up as many memories for Preston as it did for her. She stepped forward until she stood at his side. "You okay?"

"I am." He surprised her by taking her hand in his and pressing a kiss to her wrist before letting go again. "We'd better sunscreen up and get this adventure under way." He winked, and this time

Mandy couldn't ignore the flutter in her chest.

~*~

Mandy gave a little squeal as Preston pushed the canoe into the water and hopped in. The boat rocked back and forth before settling. Mandy's wide eyes and the way she gripped the sides told him how nervous she was. He couldn't halt the grin on his face. "I won't capsize this boat. If I remember right, that's your specialty."

She glared at him, but there was humor twinkling in her eyes. "That was not my fault."

"Oh, I beg to differ." He picked up a paddle resting in the bottom of the boat. "If I recall correctly, you're the one who tried to reach out and retrieve the paddle you dropped. If you hadn't done that…"

"But it was *your* fault I dropped it in the first place."

A bark of laughter escaped his lips before he could stop it. "I beg your pardon?"

"You threw that fish you caught at me and scared me to death. You knew it would freak me out."

He could still picture the way she'd thrown her arms into the air and screamed. The paddle had flown out of her hands and into the water as a result. Scaring her like that hadn't been nice at the time, but his seventeen-year-old self hadn't been able to help it. Even if he'd known they'd get soaked and have to push the canoe to the riverbank, he still would've done it. His summers spending time with Mandy and her grandparents were still some of his favorite memories.

"Okay. Maybe I had a little something to do with it." He waggled his eyebrows. "You gonna help me paddle here, or am I doing this by myself?"

She released an exasperated lungful of air and picked up the other paddle.

It'd been years since they'd ridden in a canoe together, but they quickly found their rhythm as they maneuvered their way upstream against the current. Within minutes, the sounds of the river water against the canoe and the birds singing filled the air. For the first time in longer than Preston cared to admit, the stress he carried around with him fell away. His body relaxed as they continued wordlessly, working as a unit to push the canoe around rocks and paddle against the flow.

"Did you see that one?" Mandy paused in her rowing and pointed to the circle of ripples ahead of them. "That was a big fish. I'm surprised you didn't bring your pole."

Preston always enjoyed fishing from the water, but today was about Mandy and spending time with her. "Nah. I didn't want to risk a repeat performance."

"Right." She lifted the paddle in one quick motion, sending a sprinkle of water over Preston.

"Oh, you didn't just do that." He tossed his paddle into the bottom of the boat. With a hand on each side of the canoe, he rocked it back and forth.

Mandy squealed. She braced her feet against the bottom and held on to the paddle with both hands as though it might somehow help her. "Don't you dare, Preston. I swear, if you make this boat capsize, I'll..."

"You'll what?" He stopped the rocking and waited for her response. "Well?"

Her face flushed, and she rolled her eyes. "I don't know. But I'll think of something."

"I'm shaking in my boots." He grinned when she

pierced him with her patented Mandy glare. She had no idea how attractive she looked right now. The sun shone on her gorgeous hair and the worry that lately seemed permanently etched on her face had faded away. In its place, the smile that lit her eyes filled her face. It drew his attention to her mouth and the pair of pink lips that all but begged him to kiss her.

If he gave in to the temptation now, it'd guarantee a swim to the bank.

"Fine. For the sake of our lunch."

"Uh-huh."

They paddled for a while until Mandy's energy waned. Truthfully, the muscles in his own arms were burning from the exercise he wasn't used to anymore. "You ready to take a break and eat?"

"Definitely."

They got the canoe close to the bank, and Preston stepped out, the cool water going to his shin. He pulled the canoe up the bank far enough to make it easy for Mandy to avoid the mud and get a foothold on the green grass. Once she and their cooler were safe, he pulled the canoe the rest of the way out of the water and then washed his hands off in the river. "There we go. The trek back will be a whole lot easier. We can mostly sit back and relax."

"That'll be nice." They removed their life jackets and walked up the bank a short distance until they came to some shade cast by a large cypress tree. "How does this look?"

"Looks great to me. I don't know about you, but I worked up an appetite." Preston withdrew a thin blanket he'd packed in the front pocket of the soft-sided cooler and spread it out on the grass. The light breeze made it necessary for him and Mandy to work together to get it somewhat flat. Once they did, they set the cooler on one side and then sat down themselves to keep it from blowing away.

They unpacked the lunch and ate. Mandy tapped the top of her sandwich appreciatively. "What is it about being outside that makes everything taste better?"

"We should do this more often. I'd forgotten how much fun it is to get away from everything, even if for a short while." Preston took a bite and chewed thoughtfully. "The canoe worked nicely. Your grandfather always was talented."

"So are you." She looked toward the river. "I've seen some of the things you made when you worked with Papa. I think you'll make a name for yourself with Yarrow Woodworking."

That meant a lot to Preston. "I hope so. I want this business to help us get back on our feet." He almost said he hoped to one day be able to provide everything she could want but wasn't sure how Mandy would welcome such a sentiment. "We'll get there. We make a good team, you and me. We always have. We balance each other out pretty well."

He watched his wife as she nodded thoughtfully. He wanted to gather her into his arms, and the very thought had his blood pounding like crazy. This, right here, was what he'd dreamed of for years. Everything was finally coming together with Mandy and the business. He knew she cared about him. Now he had to convince her it was okay to risk her heart. *If she'll learn to love me even a fraction of how much I love her, God, we'll be okay.*

"You're right. We've always been a good team." Her gaze shifted from his face to the river and back down at the blanket they were sitting on. "We should probably get all this cleaned up and head back. I want to make sure I have enough time to take a shower before we go over to your parents' house. I'm a mess right now." She packed things back into the cooler.

"No, Mandy. You're beautiful as always."

She opened her mouth like she was about to say something and then pressed her lips together. Finally, she said, "Thank you."

She pulled the sunscreen out and they packed everything back up again without a word. Preston reapplied his sunscreen. He watched as she got her arms, legs, and face. She gathered her hair and pulled it over one shoulder before trying to twist her arm to get the back of her neck and shoulders. He stepped forward and took the spray can from her. "Here, let me get it."

With one hand on her upper arm, he made sure her neck and shoulders were protected from the sun. The coconut sunscreen mixed with the scent of her shampoo and sun-warmed hair. He kept his hand on her arm.

"Preston?" Her voice was low, and she continued to face away from him. "Do you regret getting married?"

"No. It's one of the best decisions I've ever made." He dropped the sunscreen to the grass at his feet and gently ran a finger across the back of her shoulder. She shivered as goose bumps appeared on her skin. "The only thing I do regret is promising to not kiss you on the mouth again." He softly touched his lips to the back of her neck. Then he moved around her until he was looking into her eyes. "Because that's all I want to do right now."

She pulled her lower lip in between her teeth, and Preston groaned from the torture of not being able to taste her lips himself. Mandy's gaze dropped, and he cupped her face in his hands, lifting her eyes back to his.

"I love you, Mandy. I always have. Please believe I will never intentionally hurt you."

Chapter Eleven

Mandy let Preston's words wash over her. She'd known he cared by the way he watched over her and went out of his way to make sure she was all right. To hear him say it, though... She didn't know whether to lean into him or run away. Her emotions warred as panic set in. What if she never returned the love he offered? Or even worse, what if she fell in love with him and he changed his mind? She didn't think she could handle it now if he walked away, much less if she let her emotions surface. Keeping them buried was the safest thing.

But the walls she'd put up cracked a little with the sensation of his hands on her face. The depths of understanding in his eyes begged her to trust him. To trust herself. But after everything she'd been through and seen, how was she supposed to do that?

Even as her mind insisted she take a step back and put some distance between them, her heart had her leaning closer. She shook her head, but Preston used a thumb to softly caress her cheek. "Trust me, Mandy."

Her heart slammed against her ribs. What would it be like to let go, even if just for a few minutes, and trust Preston like he asked her to? Her eyelids lowered, her lashes pulling a veil over his face. She let herself move forward until her lips touched his. The contact was light as a feather, yet it sent electricity careening wildly through her body and stole her breath.

The kiss lasted only a moment. Preston rested his forehead against hers and when she opened her eyes, she found him watching her as though afraid she might bolt. When she didn't move, he tilted his head and covered her lips with his in a kiss full of emotion and promise, as if he were pouring his love into her. His hand shifted to the back of her head, cupping it gently. Her arms moved as if they had minds of their own, her hands clasping behind his neck.

That peck of a kiss when they were teens had affected her more than she'd ever been willing to admit—even to herself. But this one rocked her to her core, further shaking the foundation of the walls she'd built up around her emotions.

Preston pulled back, a little smile on his face and wonder in his eyes.

Mandy took a breath and a tentative step away from him. "I'm scared, Preston."

"I know, baby." He pulled her into his arms then, holding her gently. "We'll take it as slow as you want, okay?"

She nodded against his chest, and he pressed a kiss to her shoulder.

He released her then but captured her hand in his. "Come on, let's head back home. What do you say?"

"I think that sounds good."

They rode the current back down the river, only using the paddles to help steer around rocks in some of the shallower parts of the river. The whole way, Mandy compared the ride to her life. Her future.

It was easy to steer around the rocks they could see. But every once in awhile, the bottom or side of the canoe would bump into an obstacle hidden beneath the water. And when that happened, she'd suck in a breath and grip the paddle even harder, hoping it wouldn't send them into the river. It hadn't so far, but they still had to prepare. That's why their cell phones were sealed away in a waterproof container and the cooler tied to the side of the canoe. That's why they wore life jackets. Because the truth was, they couldn't guarantee a smooth ride, no matter how much they prepared.

Preston promised he'd stay forever. He could promise he'd always love her. But what if one of those unforeseen complications arose and shook their relationship badly enough to capsize them? Kissing him earlier only proved to her how easy it would be to tear those walls down and let herself love Preston. If only she could guarantee they'd steer through life's complications safely and arrive together at their destination.

She pushed the depressing thought into the back of her mind. The sun's heat was starting to get to her and rivulets of sweat made their way along her spine. She looked forward to getting cleaned up and soaking in some air conditioning by the time the dock came into view.

Preston got them to the bank and offered Mandy a hand to help her to her feet. She took it, the contact sending thoughts of their kisses through her brain.

"If you want to leave your life jacket here, I'll get

everything cleaned up. You go get a shower. I'll be inside in a while." The warm smile he gave her made Mandy's pulse skitter.

"Okay, if you're sure. I can take the cooler in."

He handed it to her. "You know what? I think I'm going to build a small lean-to over there behind the workshop. It'd be a great place to store the boats."

"That'd be perfect." She paused. "Thanks, Preston. You were right, getting away for the afternoon was exactly what we needed." Her face felt flushed from the warm day and exertion of getting back onto the bank. Hopefully he couldn't tell she was blushing on top of it.

"I was right?" He pointed a thumb at his own chest. "Boy, I wish I had that on video." He gave her a wink and flashed the smile that had her heart going a mile a minute again.

She rolled her eyes good-naturedly. "Well, don't let it go to your head. It's likely an isolated incident." She stuck her tongue out at him. "I'll see you soon." With a smile, she trekked back to the house.

As was her new habit, Mandy showered in Granny's bathroom. By the time she finished, changed into a pair of jean shorts and a pink blouse, and got down to the kitchen, they had about a half hour before they needed to leave for Preston's parents' house.

The good thing about running the B&B meant there were always pastries sitting around. Mandy gathered a selection of muffins into a container to take with her. She didn't exactly socialize often, but when she did, she hated to show up with nothing to contribute. Since Mrs. Yarrow had insisted she had everything taken care of for dinner, Mandy figured she'd take muffins the couple could eat tomorrow for breakfast.

She'd just gone over her calendar and the bookings for the coming week when Preston came downstairs. He looked ruggedly handsome in his tan cargo shorts and a black shirt with an eagle on it. His hair was wet from his shower and the smile he gave her hinted at a secret only the two of them knew.

Mandy still felt the way his lips had caressed hers and the memory shot her heart rate through the roof. As if it were a shield, she held the bag of muffins up in front of her. "I thought I'd bring something for your parents."

"I'm sure they'll appreciate it. You ready to go?"

"Absolutely." Hopefully she sounded convincing. She'd been to his parents' house a couple of times when she was a teen and she got along with them fine. But this was different. She was going to their house as their new daughter-in-law and had no idea what to expect.

~*~

Preston glanced at Mandy as he drove them to his parents' house. She'd never been one of the most talkative people he'd known, but she was too quiet right now. Was it because of their kiss? She'd responded to it by melting in his arms, hopefully a sign it affected her as much as it had him. Personally, simply thinking about the kiss only made him want to kiss her again. It was better than anything he had imagined and completely worth the wait. He hoped he wouldn't have to wait as long for the next one.

Mandy picked at her thumbnail, and Preston put a hand over hers. "You don't have to be nervous. You know my parents. They haven't changed."

"Maybe not. But we have."

"No. Our situation has. There's a difference." A glance at her told him she wasn't convinced. "They've always liked you, Mandy. Ever since the first time you came to our house to watch a movie. Do you remember that?"

She turned her head enough to give Preston a clear view of the smile on her face. "Yeah, I remember. That alien jumped out, and I threw my box of Junior Mints in the air. They flew everywhere." She chuckled. "I was mortified until we turned the lights on and your mom had done the same thing with her popcorn."

Preston laughed. "We found kernels and the occasional candy for weeks after that. It was the funniest thing ever."

Mandy nudged him with her elbow. "I'm glad we entertained you."

He drew her hand to his mouth for a light kiss and released it. He wanted to tell her that he truly enjoyed every moment he spent with her. Instead, he kept his mouth shut and drove the rest of the way in silence.

Once there, it only took about ten minutes for Mandy to relax and become more herself. They all visited in the living room for a little while until Mom stood. "I'd better go finish getting dinner ready. Shouldn't take long."

Mandy got to her feet. "I'd be happy to help you, Mrs. Yarrow."

Mom and Dad exchanged a look. "Please, Mandy. We're family now. You can call us Ellen and Stanley." She gave Mandy a little hug. "And I'd love help. Thank you."

Preston watched the women disappear, already missing his wife. He turned his attention to Dad. "How are you feeling?"

"Right as rain." Dad patted his belly. While the guy had never been heavy, he'd definitely gained weight around the middle since his transplant surgery. It was only exaggerated when Dad puffed it out as far as he could. "Fat and happy. Can't complain about that."

"No, you sure can't. I'm glad to hear it."

"How are you doing, son?"

They talked about the new business until Mom announced dinner was on the table.

The roast, potatoes, and carrots hit the spot. There wasn't a lot of talking as everyone dove into their meals. About halfway through, Mandy's cell phone rang. She withdrew it from her pocket and scowled.

Preston couldn't quite see who it was on the screen. "Something wrong?"

"I'm pretty sure it's Mr. Vincent again."

Preston held a hand out. "I'll take care of it." She handed him the phone, and he answered it. "Hudson B&B, how can I help you?"

"Yes, this is Grayson Vincent with Vincent Land. I was calling to speak to Miss Hudson. She expressed an interest in selling the place, and I was returning her call."

It was bad enough the guy kept harassing Mandy, but the outright lie made Preston angry. He pushed his chair away from the table and went to look out the window, half wishing he'd see the guy there so he could punch him. "This is Preston Yarrow. Mandy and I recently got married. I know for a fact Mrs. Yarrow is not interested in selling the place and she's told you that before. Stop calling and harassing my wife,

Vincent, or I'll be forced to visit your office next week to speak on the matter."

Complete silence. Preston looked at the phone screen to see if Mr. Vincent had hung up when his greasy voice spoke up again. "That won't be necessary. I apologize for the misunderstanding, Mr. Yarrow. Have a good evening."

Preston said nothing and hung up. He returned to the table and handed the phone back to Mandy. "Please let me know if he calls you again. He's trying to manipulate us into selling, and I won't have him harassing you."

Mandy took the phone and put it back in her pocket, her brows wrinkled. "Thanks."

Dad used a knife to put a little more butter on his potatoes. "I'm surprised people are still calling you about that. I thought they would've gotten the word you weren't selling by now."

Mandy used her fork to move some of her food around but didn't take a bite. "I'm pretty sure I've told every company in the state the B&B isn't for sale. Apparently, some individuals take a lot more convincing and won't take no for an answer."

"Well, I think that's terrible. Losing someone is hard enough without having all these people trying to buy your place out from under you." Mom gave Mandy a sympathetic smile. "I'm sorry you're having to deal with that."

"I appreciate it, Mrs. Ya — Ellen. Hopefully that'll be the last time we hear from Vincent Land."

A fresh wave of protectiveness surged through Preston as he watched Mandy. Oh, it'd better be the last time if Mr. Vincent knew what was good for him.

Mom stood and retrieved an envelope from a

nearby bookshelf. "I got these back from the photographer the other day. I hope you both don't mind that I had copies printed for you."

Preston made sure his hands were clean before he took the envelope and pulled out the pictures from their wedding. He and Mandy flipped through them. The photographer did a great job of capturing candid photos. There was even one of them talking by the tree shortly after the ceremony. His favorite picture showed him kissing her hand after they were pronounced husband and wife. Mandy watched him, her eyes full of surprise, and a little smile on her face.

Mandy reached a hand out to touch the image. "These are great, Ellen and Stanley. Thank you both so much for doing this."

Mom and Dad both smiled. "It was our pleasure. That was one of my favorites, too. I had several copies of it printed in the smaller size. Like I said, the photographer has all the files and more can be printed if you'd like. I put his card in there. You should find a nice photo album to put the images in."

Preston nudged Mandy gently with his elbow. "We'll do that."

~*~

"Did you have fun tonight?" Preston held the front door open for her and then closed it behind them.

"I did. Your parents are really nice." Some of the stories Stanley told them had Mandy laughing until her eyes watered. "I'm glad we went over there. We'll have to do that again sometime soon."

"I know they'd like that." He checked his watch.

"It's late. Are you heading to bed?"

"Not yet. I've got some online work I need to do first." She went into the kitchen, filled a glass full of water, and grabbed a bag of sugar snap peas out of the fridge. Whenever she had to stay up late to work, she got the munchies. Especially if she were going to be up for a while as she suspected she would be tonight. At least the peas would be better than snacking on something less healthy like the bag of M&Ms in the pantry calling her name. Mandy turned the light off with her elbow and Preston got the one in the living room.

He followed her upstairs and paused outside her room. "This is the third night this week, isn't it?"

Mandy set the water and peas on her dresser and turned. "Yes. But it can't be helped. I've taken on four new clients, and there's never enough time during the day to get everything done." She frowned. It might've been sweet of him to worry about her, but the disapproving look on his face only put her on the defensive. "What?"

"There's only so much one person can do. You're going to make yourself sick at this rate. If you're even half as tired as I am after today…" His voice trailed off. "You don't need to overload yourself with clients. If we pool resources together, there'll be enough money to help cushion the B&B a little."

Preston was just trying to help. He was right, too, because she was sore and tired after their canoe adventure earlier today. Mandy knew all of this, yet still resisted his suggestion. "We don't have to do that."

He crossed his arms and leaned against the doorway. "Why?"

"I can take care of this. I don't need your help,

Preston." The moment the words left her mouth, Mandy regretted saying them.

Preston straightened as though she'd struck him. His eyes flashed. "Yes, Mandy, you do. But until you can put aside your pride and accept it, I'm stuck watching you work yourself into the ground." The anger in his face gave way to sadness. He gave a little shrug, turned, and walked away as he pulled her door closed behind him.

Mandy's head began to pound, only adding one more complaint to the pains in her muscles and the ache in her heart. She was doing all of this for her grandparents. For herself. Why couldn't Preston understand that?

Chapter Twelve

Mandy slid the large metal bowl closer to Raven. They were busy slicing apples for the fritters Mandy planned to put in the oven that afternoon. She didn't remember the last time Granny had made them, but something reminded her of them the other day and she'd been craving the pastries ever since.

Raven stopped chopping, her knife poised above another red apple. "So, is there anything else we need to pull this shindig together?"

"Invitations were mailed and the RSVPs are rolling in. Tricia's thirty-four weeks along and getting bored staying indoors with this heat. It's perfect timing for a baby shower."

"Sounds good. I'll get decorations in the next day or two."

"Great. I've got the food planned out and will help you decorate before the party." Mandy grinned as she thought about their best friend. "I can't wait until she has Jasmine. This is as close as I'll ever get to having a niece."

"Do you think Tricia would hit me if I did the shower in a princess theme and bought her baby a stuffed tiger?" Raven feigned an innocent look.

Mandy flung an apple peel at her. "Don't you dare. Jasmine is a beautiful name."

"I'm joking, and yes, it is." She used both hands to scoop up her pile of apples and deposit them in the bowl. "I guess you'll be next to have a baby."

The words instantly set Mandy's cheeks blazing. "Raven, you know well why we got married."

"Yes. But have you looked at your husband lately? I don't see how you spend every day with a man like that and not want to change the stipulations of your marriage." Raven gave an exaggerated wink.

Mandy's gaze flew to the back door. The last thing she needed was for Preston to walk in right now while they were talking. "Raven!"

"Don't tell me you haven't thought about it. I guarantee you *he* has."

As if she couldn't get more embarrassed. "You are far too outspoken for your own good. Has anyone told you that before?"

"You. At least a dozen times." Raven watched her as though she were waiting for some kind of confession.

Okay, maybe Mandy had thought about the kiss a million times since their outing. And maybe her thoughts were in a constant battle between wishing he'd kiss her again and hoping he wouldn't. But ever since their argument the other night, it'd all been a non-issue anyway. They got along okay, but the easy camaraderie between them had disappeared. Mandy hated it. It was as if they were at an impasse with both waiting for the other one to make the first move.

Raven was still staring at her, and Mandy was well aware Raven wouldn't let it go until Mandy confessed to *something*.

"We kissed on Saturday."

Raven leaned forward as though Mandy had revealed the most interesting piece of gossip in years. "And?"

"It was amazing and scary all rolled into one." That was an understatement.

"What happened after that?"

"We argued about money that night and everything's been weird ever since." When Mandy said it like that, the whole thing seemed lame. She told Raven about their conversation.

Raven looked thoughtful a moment before she leaned back in her chair. "You realize he's just trying to help you, right?"

"Yes, I do." Mandy tossed several apple slices into the bowl harder than was necessary. "But I told him I had it handled, and he got offended." Raven stared at her and Mandy finally set her knife down and sighed. "What? Just spit it out."

"You're working all hours of the day and night. It sounds to me like you could use some help. Men like to fix things, Mandy. Preston's been doing that for your family for years. He married you to help you keep this place, for crying out loud. Why are you pushing him away now?"

Mandy rolled her eyes. "I thought you were supposed to be on my side."

"I am. I'm looking out for you. And you, my friend, are far too stubborn for your own good. Maybe he doesn't understand why it's so important for you to handle everything yourself. Frankly, neither do I."

Raven always did tell it like it was. Mandy groaned and cradled her head in her hands. "So, what am I supposed to do?"

"Figure out what you really want. If you'd rather he left you alone, I think you've probably accomplished that task pretty well. Or, if you want him to kiss you again, you're going to have to mend fences and take some initiative. Because if Preston is one thing, he's a gentleman."

Raven was right. The poor guy didn't know where they stood. Good grief, *she* didn't know where they stood. But the weirdness between them the last day and a half had to end. They needed to talk about it. Kiss again. Something. And she was probably way over-thinking the whole blasted thing.

It was time to change the topic. Or at least turn the focus on something besides herself. "What about you? Have any handsome princes snagged your attentions as of late?"

Raven's laugh filled the kitchen. "Oh, no. I'm not holding my breath waiting for someone to come and sweep me off my feet." Her voice was strong, but there was a vulnerability in her eyes. "I've got my job at the rehab center and two of the best friends in the world. Who needs romance?"

Mandy wasn't fooled. Raven had always had a big personality and a take-charge mentality, both of which scared guys off a little. They were the same personality points that made her such a great physical therapist, though. "There's a guy somewhere just waiting for you. He'll show up when you least expect it."

"Like I said, I'm not holding my breath." Raven finished slicing the last apple, gathered the peels for the trash, and rinsed the knife off in the sink. "Do me a favor and save me one of these fritters."

"You're welcome to hang out until they're done if you want to."

"I wish I could, but I have patients later this afternoon, and I'd better get going." Raven dried her hands off on a towel and then gave Mandy a quick hug. "Your prince is right here under your nose. He's the guy who told Grady to lay off when he kept teasing you our sophomore year. Preston was the one who helped you glue your science experiment back together again after you dropped it in the hall. And it's because of him you still have your grandparents' place. Don't forget that, okay?"

"Yeah, I know."

"Then apologize and kiss him again, already!"

"Unless you want me to put you to work actually making the fritters, I suggest you quit harassing me."

Raven lifted both hands and grinned. "I'm out of here. Baking is on my short list of torturous activities. You have fun, and I'll talk to you later."

"See you."

As much as Mandy wanted to shake off her friend's words, she couldn't. It was true, Preston had always been there for her. When she was a freshman, he'd gone out of his way to say hi or help when he could.

Good grief, the guy had even married her to get her out of a scrape. Granted, it helped him, too. But still. All her life, things had been such a mess she'd been forced to rely on others. First her grandparents to give her a home, her few friends to get her through school, and now Preston to keep her from losing her home. Would she ever get to the point where she didn't need someone to save her?

~*~

"You've got to be kidding me!"

Mandy's words and the frustration in her voice were the first things Preston registered when he walked in through the back door. "Mandy? What's wrong?"

She came into the kitchen, her posture stiff, and both hands up in the air. "Our air conditioner's not working. And, of course, I don't notice until it gets warm in here and it's," she gestured indignantly at the clock above the stove, "after five o'clock. No one will be able to fix anything until Monday."

The house hadn't seemed that bad when Preston first walked in, especially compared to the high-nineties outside. Now that he'd been inside for a few minutes, he could tell it would get stifling hot, and fast. Especially upstairs. "Have you tried calling in case someone is working late?"

"Two of them. I'm about to call a few more. They've all expressed their regret but say they can't get here until sometime on Monday."

"Okay, you keep calling and I'll see if I can figure out what's going on."

"The fan keeps running, but it's putting out warm air. I had someone come and service the unit in April. We shouldn't be having any problems."

"I'll check on it. How many guests do we have tonight?"

"One room is rented out." She clenched her jaw, worry in her eyes.

She'd already been on edge since their disagreement the other night. The last thing they needed was to have these guests leave and demand a

119

refund. "Keep calling. I'll be right back."

There didn't appear to be anything wrong with the part of the unit inside the house, but when he checked on the compressor outside, the issue was immediately apparent. The line was frozen solid. There wasn't anything he could do, so he headed back inside.

Mandy was still on the phone with someone, but by the dejected look on her face, the news wasn't good. "Yeah. I understand. Thank you anyway." She hung up. "I've got someone coming first thing Monday morning, but that's the earliest anyone committed to. Any luck?"

He shook his head. "I wish I had better news. The line is frozen and the compressor is overheating. They may have serviced it, but I think it's out of coolant, which probably means a leak. We may as well turn the A/C off because it'll just keep running indefinitely otherwise."

Two hours later, their guests had opted for a hotel in town. There was nothing Mandy could do but give them the refunds they requested. She texted Jade and Elise to let them know they didn't need to come in until Monday.

By seven o'clock, Preston and Mandy were the only people left in the house. Preston walked up behind her as she checked the thermostat for the temperature. "It feels a lot warmer than eighty-two, doesn't it?" Sweat trickled down his back. "I can't believe it's so warm. The weatherman on the radio this morning said this should be one of the last heatwaves for the year."

"I sure hope that's the case. I think it's probably five degrees hotter upstairs. No way can we sleep up there tonight."

"I'm sure my parents would let us stay with them over the weekend."

She objected immediately. "I'd rather not. I don't want to put them out." Her stomach let loose a long growl and she sighed. "I forgot about dinner."

"I'll order us a pizza. You go take a shower while I see what I can do to get the living room cooled down." She looked dubious. Preston put his hands on her shoulders and steered her toward the stairs. "I'm serious."

"Okay."

After getting dinner ordered, Preston went to Mandy's room to retrieve her box fan. He stopped when he entered her room. There, on the side table, was a picture of them from their wedding. When had she framed it? He smiled. With her fan in one hand and his own oscillating fan in the other, he headed downstairs. He opened the front door and slid the glass on the screen door upwards, letting in the slightly cooler night air. Then he set both fans in front of the screen. It wasn't much, but it was better than nothing. Finally, he found a spare sheet, wet it in the kitchen sink, and draped the damp fabric over the front of the box fan. The difference was immediate and Preston stood in front of it for several moments, relishing the cooling effect on his sweaty skin.

"Wow, that already feels better."

He turned to find Mandy walking into the room, her wet hair hanging past her shoulders. The knit shorts and tank top looked a lot cooler but ratcheted his own body temperature up ten degrees. He swallowed hard. "We may want to sleep in here tonight. You can take the couch, and I can crash on the recliner."

She looked like she might object. But when she stopped in front of the fan and closed her eyes with relief, she quickly agreed. "You're probably right."

Preston couldn't take his gaze off her as she enjoyed the cool air. "I'm sorry this happened tonight. I know it's the last thing you needed right now."

Her long eyelashes lifted to reveal eyes filled with uncertainty. "I need to apologize for the other night. You were only looking out for me, and I threw it back in your face." She paused. "I'm not very good at accepting help from people."

"You're not kidding." He slipped his hands into his pockets and raised an eyebrow. One side of his mouth quirked upward. "As much as you like to think otherwise, we're in this together. What happens to the B&B affects me, just like changes to the woodworking business affect you."

"I know." She ran her fingers through her hair and sighed. "I hate needing help in the first place."

"Yeah, you're stubborn like that." He winked at her.

Mandy chuckled. "You're not the first person to tell me that today."

"That's because it's true."

She reached for a nearby magazine and tossed it at him. "Whatever."

The heavy awkwardness that had existed between them since Sunday night dissipated. Preston still wasn't happy with Mandy's need to handle everything herself, but at least they were talking again even if he wasn't completely sure where they stood.

A car approached the house, the headlights nearly blinding them. Preston dug his wallet out of his pocket. "That must be the pizza."

"Thank goodness, I'm starved. I'll go grab the plates."

It felt good to kick back in the recliners, turn on some TV, and eat. The fans worked to slowly cool the room from a self-combusting level to one that was at least somewhat tolerable. If it hadn't, he might have suggested they camp out in the workshop for the night. It had its own air conditioning unit, and he'd checked it while outside to make sure it was still working.

He moved from the recliner to the couch where he sat against the corner between the arm and the back and stretched his legs out along the cushions. He glanced at Mandy. She was still watching TV, but her eyelids looked heavy. At least she seemed relaxed. "Since the workshop will be cooled off tomorrow, do you want to come work on your grandfather's canoe with me?"

She turned to look at him. "With no guests, there's nothing for me to do here." Her voice held a tinge of sarcasm. She seemed to realize how she sounded and flinched. "I'm sorry. I'm exhausted. It's been one of those days. Yes, I think spending the day in the workshop sounds like a great idea."

"Awesome." The prospect of having time with her brightened his whole night.

The TV program ended and Mandy took the plates and leftover pizza into the kitchen. He heard her check the back door and then she turned out the kitchen lights. She stopped at the base of the stairs. "I need a few things from my room. I'll be right back."

It was after eleven. No wonder they were both beat. Preston went upstairs to change into a pair of shorts and a T-shirt. He snagged his pillow off the bed and headed back to the main floor. He found Mandy spreading a thin blanket out on the couch. She handed another one to him. "It's wishful thinking, but I brought them just in case."

"Thanks." He took it and draped it over his arm.

"You sure you're okay on the recliner?"

"Absolutely."

"Okay." She fidgeted with her thumb and then clasped her hands together behind her back.

Mandy looked uncertain and clearly needed a rescue. As much as he wanted to take her in his arms for a proper kiss, Preston leaned forward and only brushed one against her cheek.

They dimmed the living room lights. Preston got himself set up in the recliner and leaned it back as far as it would go. He was just starting to relax when Mandy's voice broke the silence.

"Preston?"

"Yeah?"

A pause. "Thanks for looking out for me. I don't like needing help from anyone, but I promise I'll try not to be as much of an idiot about it."

Preston chuckled. "I'm glad. Get some rest, Mandy. I'll see you in the morning."

"You, too. Good night."

The last day and a half had been near torture, but they'd made some progress tonight. The sound of the fans in the background and thoughts of Mandy eventually lulled Preston to sleep.

Chapter Thirteen

Mandy woke slowly Saturday morning, and she took a minute to remember where she was. The fans still ran in front of the screen door. While not technically chilly, she noted that, at some point last night, she'd pulled the light blanket up to cover herself. She shifted on the couch and found Preston watching her with a small smile on his face.

She startled a little. "It's kind of creepy to have you sitting there staring at me."

He chuckled, his deep voice soothing. "I woke up maybe a minute before you did, if it helps any. So, I was only creepy for sixty seconds."

Mandy couldn't keep her own laughter at bay. She sat up and ran her fingers through her hair. "Did you sleep okay?"

He brought the recliner to an upright position and groaned loudly. His movements were slow as he stood up. "I definitely prefer it to passing out from heat exhaustion upstairs. How about you?"

"Truthfully? I may have slept better last night

than I have since Granny passed." The confession surprised even her. Why had she slept so well? Was it because she hadn't slept upstairs where she kept expecting to hear Granny walk down the hall? Or because she was in the same room as Preston, and he made her feel safe? Unwilling to examine the reasons much longer for fear of discovering the uncomfortable truth, she changed the subject. "I suggest we change, eat breakfast, and get out to the workshop before it gets much warmer. We can have sandwiches for lunch so we don't have to cook and heat the place up much."

"And I'd like to take you out for dinner and a movie tonight." Preston had thrown that out there so smoothly it took a minute for Mandy to process it. He must have thought she'd object—and she probably would have—because he held up a hand to stop her. "Both places will be air conditioned. Then we can come back tonight, put the fans in front of the screen again, and we won't have to be miserably hot any more than necessary today."

It made sense. Besides, after spending little time together in the last couple of days, Mandy had to admit she was looking forward to spending the day with him. "Okay."

His surprise at her agreement quickly changed to satisfaction. "Meet you back down here in a few."

Not much later, they grabbed some muffins and headed out. It was warming up outside, and Mandy was glad to have a cool place to spend the day. The moment they entered the workshop, the scent of cedar enveloped her. It reminded her of Papa, and she stopped. How many times had she gone in to tell him lunch was ready, to find him running the band saw or sanding down a piece of wood? Her breath caught in her throat and tears stung the back of her eyes.

"Mandy?"

Preston's voice made her jump. She sniffed and blinked her eyes rapidly to rid them of the moisture. "Yeah. Sorry. There are a lot of memories here."

"I'm the one who's sorry. If you'd rather not stay out here today, I'd understand."

"No." She walked to the old wooden chair her grandfather had kept in the workshop for as long as she remembered and ran a hand over the back. "They're good memories. I guess I wasn't prepared for them."

He brushed his lips against the top of her head and gave her hand a squeeze. "I'm proud of you."

"I'm glad you kept this chair." She sat down in it, enjoying the cool touch of the wood against her arms. "I used to sit here and wait for Papa to finish working and come in to eat." She pointed to one of the big gouges in the right arm. "This one was my fault, you know. It was the first year I came to live here." She glanced at Preston to find he was watching her with interest. "I had a screwdriver and a piece of discarded wood. I was determined to carve my name into it. Except the screwdriver slipped and went right into the arm of the chair." She chuckled. "I was certain Papa would send me away."

"And, of course, he didn't. What did he say?"

She smiled. "He said, 'Mandy girl, mistakes are an important part of life. The key is to learn your lesson the first time.' Then he showed me how to use the correct tools to carve my name. I still have that piece of wood in my room."

"That's a great memory. Your grandfather was a special man." The thoughtful look on his face turned to one of concern. "I don't think I've ever seen you cry, Mandy. Not even when you fell and cut your leg on the rock by the river."

Mandy stretched her leg out and ran a finger down the two-inch scar next to her knee. She and Preston had been trying to use a tree trunk to cross the river. She'd almost gotten across when she slipped and fell near the bank. The memory of the pain was still as sharp as the rock she'd fallen on. "I don't like to cry."

"Why? Sometimes it can be therapeutic." He grabbed an old barstool and brought it closer before straddling it to face her.

Mandy couldn't quite meet his eyes. Instead, she focused on the little shavings of wood littering the concrete floor at her feet. "My mom used to yell at me when I cried. She told me it was a sign of weakness. That anyone who saw me cry would think I was a pathetic little girl." Her mother's words used to echo in Mandy's head when she was young. Over the years, she'd learned to tune them out. But some of the hurtful things that were said never faded away completely. "So, I didn't cry in front of my parents. And eventually, I got used to not crying, even when I was alone."

Preston's face looked pained and sadness filled his gray eyes. "I'm sorry you grew up like that, Mandy. I hope you know what your mother told you was anything but the truth."

"I do realize that. But it's hard to shake." She shrugged. There wasn't anything else to say. She sniffed. "So, show me what you've been up to out here. I need to take pictures of you working for the website." She got the impression he was allowing the change in subject, though he didn't look convinced.

"I was hoping to get a lot of things listed for sale

on Monday." He showed her the intricate coaster sets he'd made, each crafted from different shades of wood pieced together to create beautiful patterns. There were also several full-size paddles he'd crafted along with smaller ones meant to be displayed. Each one was unique. Carved wooden measuring spoons and cutting boards sat displayed on another table.

"Wow, Preston. These are amazing." She ran a hand over one of the cutting boards. Granny would've loved something like this. "I bet you could etch in the town's name on a lot of these and sell them to all the people who come to the area to camp."

He nodded. "I'd thought of that, too. These are to sell online, and I didn't want them tied to one place."

Preston showed her the canoe Papa had crafted over the years. "I remember watching him make this one." He put his palm against the canoe. "I was fascinated by the whole process and excited when he said I could help with the next one." He smiled with the memory. "Your grandfather was a kind and patient man to let a bored kid come in and help him build. That's why I want to finish the last canoe he was working on." He pointed to the cloth-covered shape by the wall.

Mandy ran a hand over the smooth cedar of the canoe. The boats shone, the tones warm and inviting. Papa loved creating things by hand, and she was glad Preston felt the same way.

"Papa would be proud of you."

Preston's eyes developed a sheen. He smiled at her. "I appreciate that." He cleared his throat. "Okay, let's get to work. What do you say?"

~*~

Preston took the cloth cover off the unfinished canoe, revealing the work-in-progress lying top-down across the long, narrow wooden work table. "I finished stripping the hull yesterday. Now that the glue is dry, I can trim the strips to make them flush at the bow and stern."

He remembered when Mr. Hudson had explained all of this to him years ago. It seemed strange to be doing the same for Mandy. "Did your grandfather ever show you how he built his boats?"

"No. I guess I wasn't interested back then." There was a hint of regret in her voice. "I've seen them in various stages of completion, but that's about it." She looked thoughtful. "You know what? Go ahead and do that. I think I'll go get my camera and laptop. Maybe I can take pictures of what you've made and even add some products to the website while you work."

Preston grinned. "That's a great idea."

He trimmed the strips, admiring the way the canoe was finally taking shape. Until now, it looked odd and boxy. Once the bow and stern were more defined, the streamlined look of the canoe was revealed. This was one of his favorite parts of the building process.

Mandy came back into the workshop and closed the door behind her to keep out the heat. He helped her find a place to plug her laptop in and get set up nearby. She blinked at the canoe. "Wow, you got that done fast."

"That part doesn't take long. Next, I can remove the staples." He pointed to a mason jar sitting on one of the work benches. "Can you hand that to me, please?"

"Sure." Mandy retrieved the jar and gave it to him. "That's a lot of staples to pull out."

"It is. And I have to do it carefully because cedar is a soft wood, and I don't want to make dents in it." One by one, he took each staple out of the hull and dropped it into the jar with a clink. When he'd finished, he ran a gloved hand over the wood.

"Wow. It's almost like magic, the way it transforms." Mandy stood nearby, her Canon camera in her hand. "What are you going to do now?"

"Come here," he beckoned. When she was next to him, he took her hand and placed it on the wood. "Can you feel those bumps where the strips meet? I need to use a plane and smooth it out. Especially at the bow and stern. Once everything's evened off, then we can start sanding."

"We?" She looked surprised.

"I thought I'd teach you how." Just having her in the workshop with him was amazing. Working together, side by side, appealed to him more than he'd thought possible. Suddenly, the need for her to want the same was so strong, he held his breath as he waited for her response.

"I have no idea what I'm doing, but I'd be happy to try."

He exhaled with a smile. "Great! Using the plane to smooth the hull out will probably take a while. You can take pictures of everything else for now if you want to."

"Sure. And I thought I might take a few of you working as well. It'd be good to show you in action on the website. Do you mind?"

"I think that's a great idea."

She nodded, all business. Preston focused on what he was doing as he worked on the hull, vaguely aware of the sounds of the shutter as Mandy took photos. Twenty minutes later, she ran a cord from her camera to the computer and sat back down again.

They worked in companionable silence for a while. Preston usually ended up putting some music on his phone when he was alone to help fill the void. Today, however, there was no need to do that. Being with Mandy and their occasional chitchat was more than enough.

He smoothed everything out as much as possible with the plane and set it aside. He shook his arms, trying to work the tightness from his muscles. Mandy focused on her computer screen, her brows drawn together in concentration. When she fiddled with one of her thumbnails, Preston chuckled. That brought her gaze right to his.

She gave him a tentative smile. "What?"

The woman had no idea how gorgeous she was. Or how cute she looked when she was concentrating. The fact she didn't know was yet one more reason why he cared so much about her. She'd never been one of those stuck-up girls in school who tried to outdo everyone else. She was just Mandy. Sweet, considerate, and breathtakingly beautiful. Love swelled in his chest as his heart turned over.

"You're cute when you're focused. And even cuter when you get embarrassed."

Mandy's cheeks turned bright pink. She grabbed a paintbrush off the table next to her and tossed it at him. "Preston!" She looked down at her computer, her hair falling to create a curtain that hid her face. There was no missing the way her lips curved up at the corners, though.

He remembered their kiss last week and desperately wanted another. He didn't want to push her, and it wasn't like she'd made it clear she'd welcome another kiss. So here they were. He wished he knew if the whole thing was making her as crazy as it was him.

Preston pulled the barstool beside her chair and took a seat. "How's the website coming along?"

"So far, so good." She turned the laptop allowing him to see the screen more. "I'm creating a page to show some of the process. I want people to see every piece you make is handcrafted and unique. It makes it seem more personal. Plus, people will be more willing to pay higher prices if they know what kind of craftsmanship goes into them."

He admired the page, and they talked about several layout options. It gave him the break his arms needed, and he enjoyed working together with her on the site. "You ready to learn how to sand?" He stood up and held a hand out to her.

She didn't look overly sure of herself, but she closed the laptop, set it down, and reached for his hand. "Ready as I'll ever be. I don't want to ruin the boat."

"You won't." He gave her hand a squeeze and let go. He retrieved the electric sander, placed a new piece of sandpaper on it, and then plugged it into the nearby outlet. "The key to sanding the hull is to run the sander all over the surface until the whole hull is smooth to the touch. And while I was careful to remove all the staples, keep an eye out for any I may have missed." She was hanging onto his every word, her eyes wide. "Okay, let me show you first, and then you can try. If you get the hang of it, we have more than one sander and we can double team this."

He took several minutes to smooth a section of the hull, moving the sander evenly over the surface before proceeding to another area. Then he motioned for her to take the sander. Preston positioned himself behind her, a hand over hers, and guided her movements. It took all he had to focus on the task and not the fact her face was so close to his. Her silky hair tickled his cheek and her scent filled his nose.

With a flip of the switch, he turned the sander off. Mandy immediately turned her head to try to look at him. "Did I do something wrong?"

"Yes. You figured this whole thing out way faster than I wanted you to."

She looked completely confused, and Preston had to fight to keep his neutral expression in place.

"I don't understand."

"I think you're ready to manage a sander on your own." He leaned a little closer and whispered in her ear. "But I rather prefer helping you out like this." If he'd wanted to kiss her before, that need had risen tenfold. He couldn't see her face well enough to know whether she would welcome it or not. "You keep this one, and I'll plug the other sander in. We could be done with this part by lunch."

He turned to move away when she put a hand on his arm to stop him. Then she surprised him by turning partway, going on tip-toes, and placing a kiss to his cheek. "Thanks, Preston."

All he could do was grin at her in response. As they worked together the rest of the morning, he kept catching glimpses of her face. And every time she caught him watching her, she'd flush a little. But then, he also caught her watching him, and that gave him hope.

Hope that maybe, just maybe, Mandy could fall for him the way he'd fallen for her years ago.

Chapter Fourteen

Mandy didn't think she could eat another bite until the smell of warm, buttery popcorn wafted to them from an open door in the theater. No matter what, there was always room for popcorn.

Their dinner at the Italian restaurant had been amazing. The salad, soup, and breadsticks alone would've been enough, but she couldn't turn away the big plate of lasagna the waiter set down in front of her. After working all afternoon on the canoe, they'd both been ravenous. She hadn't realized how much energy went into working with her hands. No wonder it seemed like Preston would eat them out of house and home at every meal. Now her stomach was uncomfortably full.

Preston purchased tickets for the latest super hero flick. By the time they got their popcorn, drinks, and found a spot to sit, the lights were dimming and previews beginning. He leaned to his right and whispered near her ear. "We barely made it."

His nearness sent a jolt of warmth to Mandy's

middle. They were sharing popcorn. How on Earth was she supposed to follow the plot when she had to think about that every time she reached for a buttery handful?

As it turned out, their hands didn't connect as often as she thought they would. What surprised and confused her the most was the disappointment she experienced. It shouldn't matter. She was supposed to be keeping her distance and protecting herself. Because of that, she should avoid physical contact with Preston at all costs, especially when she knew exactly what it did to her.

Halfway through the movie, Mandy was a mess of jumbled nerves. She hadn't paid as much attention to the story as she should have, and she was so aware of Preston and what he was doing that she jumped whenever he moved.

They finished the popcorn, and he set the container down on the floor at their feet. She wiped her greasy hands off on a napkin and noticed he did the same thing. Then, to her shock, he reached over and took her hand in his. He leaned in close and whispered, "There, that's better." The warmth of his hand combined with a wink from him scattered the last of her focus on the movie. For the rest of the show, all that existed was Preston's touch and the alternating waves of elation and fear that kept vying for top spot in her emotions.

Once the movie finished, they walked through the parking lot in search of Preston's truck. Even though the sun had set, the warmth emanating from the pavement served as a cruel reminder of the broken air conditioner waiting for them at the house. She checked the clock on her phone and fought back a yawn. "I didn't realize how late it was." It'd be after eleven by the time they got back.

"Yeah, me, neither. It'll probably take a little while to get the living room cooled off enough to sleep. I'll get that going as soon as we get home." Preston checked for traffic and pulled out of the parking lot.

It awed Mandy how easily he'd referred to the B&B as home. The transition into marriage, a change in profession, and a complicated relationship seemed to be easy for him. Or was he just exceptionally good at hiding how he truly felt?

She studied his profile as passing cars and streetlights illuminated his face from time to time. Preston's ability to roll with the punches was the one thing she admired most about him. Would he be disappointed if he knew how difficult the whole thing had been for her? Marrying in order to keep the house and land was ridiculous. They should've gone to her directly.

Sometimes she wanted to scream about the unfairness of it all.

And yet, if it hadn't been for her grandparents putting stipulations in the will, she wouldn't be here with Preston right now.

By the time they got home, Mandy was exhausted. Preston got the fans going while she took a quick shower and changed. She curled up on her side on one end of the oversize couch to wait for Preston to return from his shower. The cool air from the fans blew over her skin. Before she knew it, her eyes drifted closed, and she fell asleep. At one point, she vaguely noticed Preston come back into the room, turn the lights off, and curl up on the opposite end of the couch.

When she woke up, she stretched her legs along the length of the couch. Remembering Preston sleeping on the other end, she sat upright, afraid she might have kicked him. His blanket and a pillow were still there, but he was nowhere to be seen.

Mandy yawned and stood with a stretch. The scent of coffee filled the air and drew her to the kitchen.

Preston looked up from the pan of scrambled eggs he was cooking. "Good morning, sleepy head. I was about to wake you."

"Good morning." She caught sight of her nearly transparent reflection in the tall window above the sink and tried to smooth her hair down. "Thanks for making breakfast."

"You're welcome. Did you sleep okay last night? I hope I didn't crowd you on the couch. The recliner totally made my back ache."

"No, it didn't bother me at all. I don't blame you."

"Good." He gave her a bright smile. "Are you up to church?"

It was Sunday. With the change in routine from the lack of guests, Mandy had lost track of time. "Sure."

"Then have yourself a seat. There's orange juice poured, and these eggs are almost done."

She did as he suggested, sitting at the bar in the middle of the kitchen. She took a sip of orange juice and watched as Preston finished the eggs and divided them between two plates. It was hard to grasp the fact that Preston, the boy she used to run with, tease, and often argue with, stood in her kitchen making her breakfast. A *lot* had happened in the last month and a half.

~*~

Mandy stared at the clock in the kitchen Monday morning. It was almost eleven. Elise had arrived moments ago, and Jade was walking in the door now.

As soon as Jade saw Mandy, she stopped and frowned. "Well, don't you look like a ray of sunshine? They didn't get the A/C fixed yet?"

"Nope." Mandy hopped down from the chair at the bar and stalked across the floor only to return again. "They told me someone would be here between eight and ten. We have guests coming this evening and need the air conditioner running again. If we get many more cancellations…" She stopped herself. With nothing else to do that morning, she'd gone over all the financials again. Truthfully, if something didn't change soon, she might have to let Elise go. Possibly Jade, too.

"Is it that bad?" The concern in Jade's eyes mirrored Elise's.

"Yeah, it is. We're barely earning enough money to keep the B&B afloat. Preston and I have been coming up with ideas to help bring in more guests. We'll even offer canoe rentals, which I think will be fun. We also have Preston's website up to help bring business, and I'd like to set up a little store inside somewhere. He's got a lot of great, one-of-a-kind things guests might want to buy to remember their stay here. But none of it matters if we can't get the guests here and keep them."

Jade and Elise both looked grim. The three women waited in silence, the ticking of the clock echoing through the room. Still no sign of the mechanic.

"You know," Jade began, "if you need to find some extra income, you could always turn your breakfasts into more of a pastry deal. Use your grandmother's recipes and even bake a day ahead. I'd understand if you need to terminate my employment here. I just do it for fun, anyway, now that my kids are all grown and gone."

The older woman's kind words brought a much-needed smile to Mandy's face. "I appreciate that, Jade. It may have to be a possibility. I want to give it another couple of weeks, though. See how Preston's business takes off and see if we can't bring in more guests with the boats." She put an arm around each of the ladies. "I appreciate you both and will keep you updated on what's going on."

"Thanks, Mandy." Elise looked relieved. "I realize I only work a few hours a day here, but this job has been a real blessing."

They chatted for a few minutes before Elise got to work. Jade went through the cookbook and made her notes for the week. She was walking out when a white van pulled up the driveway.

"It's about time," Mandy muttered and went out to meet them.

An hour later, wonderfully cool air blasted from the vents all around the house. Thankfully, only the tubing had been damaged and nothing else major was wrong with the compressor. Mandy wrote a check, forcing herself not to flinch at the cost of the repair, and thanked the guy.

She heard the back door open and the sound of Preston's shoes stomping on the welcome mat.

"We've got air conditioning!" His deep voice

carried into the living room.

Mandy walked into the kitchen and grinned. "Yes, thank you, Lord! The guy just left. I was getting nervous about having the place cooled off in time to welcome guests this afternoon." The relief was so strong she didn't realize she'd leaned into Preston with a half hug until his arm went around her waist and pulled her closer.

"I'm glad. And I have more good news for you." He looked down at her, his gray eyes twinkling. "I checked the online store right before coming in, and we've had two sales, plus a custom order for a kayak paddle. Not only that, but my boss from Clearwater Lumber, Mr. Logan, opened a convenience store near a couple of those popular campgrounds. He heard about the new business and wants to sell a bunch of our stuff on consignment since there are many tourists going through there. He's planning on having a display and everything."

"Are you serious?" Mandy moved back, allowing her to see his face better. "That's amazing, Preston! I'm thrilled for you. You deserve this."

"*We* deserve this," he corrected.

Mandy couldn't deny how that one word warmed her. "Hopefully things are finally changing for the better."

"I sure hope so." The delight on Preston's face morphed into something else, something more intense. He lifted a hand to run his fingers through her hair and cup the back of her neck.

The heat from his palm permeated her skin as her eyes drifted shut from the contact. When her lashes lifted again, his face was only a breath from hers. Before she allowed herself to second guess everything, she rose on her tiptoes and met his lips with hers.

He took over from there, kissing her thoroughly until they were both out of breath. The sound of someone clearing her throat finally broke them apart. Mandy's face heated when she saw Elise grinning from the doorway.

"I wanted you to know I finished everything. There wasn't a lot to do today. I'll be back tomorrow," she said, an amused look on her face.

Mandy took a sidestep away from Preston so she could think straight. "I appreciate it, Elise. Have a great rest of your Monday."

"You, too."

They could hear her laughing as she closed the door behind her.

Mandy covered her face with her hands and groaned. She split her fingers and peeked at Preston between them. There was no hint of embarrassment or regret on his face. She tried to discern what that look meant when he answered the question for her.

"I love it when you blush. I'll always be finding new ways to make that happen."

Mandy shook her head. "I think you have enough weapons in your arsenal as it is," she muttered behind her hands, unable to keep the smile from her face. "Come on, Casanova, let's get some lunch and enjoy the fact we won't melt while we're eating."

At least not from the air temperature, anyway.

Chapter Fifteen

Something woke Preston up early Wednesday morning. He turned his phone's screen on and flinched at the brightness. Two thirty-five. He held his breath and listened, but noticed nothing out of the ordinary. He doubted he'd be able to fall asleep again until he did a quick check of the house.

He pulled on a T-shirt to go with the shorts he wore, slipped some shoes on, and stepped into the hall. Mandy's room was open, but when he looked inside, her bed was empty. She had to be downstairs, and that was probably what he had heard.

He found Mandy sitting at the bar in the kitchen, her head bent over her laptop and a stack of papers at her left elbow. She wore a pair of loose pants and a flowing T-shirt, and her hair was gathered in a loose ponytail at the base of her head. She sat in the chair, one leg curled underneath. When she noticed him, her head jerked up, and she jumped a little.

"Did I wake you up? I'm sorry." She frowned. Her eyes looked tired and dark circles colored the skin below them. "I needed some tea and nearly dropped my glass."

"I heard a noise and wanted to make sure everything was okay. What are you doing up at this hour?" He crossed the kitchen to see her computer screen and a client's website open.

"I'm trying to get caught up." Mandy smothered a wide yawn with her hand. "Although I'm seeing double at this point." She rolled her shoulders back.

Preston rested his hands on her shoulders and gently massaged the muscles. They were full of knots. "Baby, you should go to bed and get some rest." His fingers itched to pull her hair from the band holding it back. He loved the way it flowed around her shoulders. He stamped down the temptation and continued to work her stressed muscles.

"Yeah." She saved the website she was working on and closed the laptop. After searching through the stack of papers, she pulled out a spiral-bound notebook. "I looked through all the finances again. I hate to do it, but if I let Elise and Jade go, I can take over their jobs. That'll save us some money right there. Then, if I pick up a few more clients for website work—"

Preston was shaking his head before she finished speaking. "And when are you going to build and maintain these websites if you're cleaning the rooms and doing all the cooking for breakfast? At two every morning? Mandy, you work like that, and you'll make yourself sick. No one can keep that kind of schedule going. Even if you do, will it dig the B&B out of a financial hole?"

Mandy's silence confirmed what he'd suspected the answer would be. His hands stilled. "The woodworking business is taking off. Did I tell you Mr. Logan called me earlier today and asked for more pieces to put in his store? Apparently, the coasters and paddles are the big sellers. I'm going to make miniature paddles and turn them into key chains."

"That's great, Preston." She turned her head and gave him a tired smile. "You've put a lot into your business. You deserve this."

Preston suppressed a sigh. She still refused to consider anything as "theirs." He'd been trying to let it go, hoping and praying she'd eventually change her way of thinking. But she was being obstinate about it, one of her personality traits that both made him love her more, and drove him absolutely insane.

He gave her shoulders a final squeeze before letting his hands drop to his sides. "How about we both sit down after church tomorrow and see where we can trim some expenses? Money's come in with the woodworking, and since we didn't have to put anything into getting the equipment, that can help balance out what we're not making with the B&B."

Mandy's back stiffened. "There has to be a way. You shouldn't have to give up your money."

Her words were like a punch to the chest. *When will you see it's our money?* But he said nothing. She wouldn't change her mind. Certainly not now when she was about to drop from exhaustion. "We won't find the answers tonight."

"I know." She groaned as she stood. "I sometimes wonder if we ever will."

Preston understood. There were times he wondered the very same thing. He took her hand in his and gently pulled her to her feet. "Come here." He led her to the living room where he sat on the couch and tugged her down next to him.

When his arms went around her, Mandy snuggled against his chest. Her breathing evened out as she started to relax.

"That's better." Preston rested his cheek against her head. "I wish I knew what the answer was. You keep thinking it's up to you to find it. I'm here too, remember? You're not alone. We're not alone. We've been so frantic to solve our own problems we haven't been bringing them to God. Or, at least I know I haven't."

Mandy tilted her head back so she could see his face. "You're right. I haven't been, either."

He kissed her forehead then tucked her head against his chest again. "Then that's what we need to do. Pray. Because there will be an answer. This can't keep going on. What we need is the wisdom to find the solution."

God, only You know what the future holds. And only You can see inside Mandy's heart. She's hurting and as much as I want to fix things for her, she won't let me. I want to pray You'll help her fall in love with me, but what she needs the most is peace. Peace from the pressures she's putting on herself. Peace from the past actions of her parents she can't seem to shake. Father, please help her move forward.

Mandy and Raven stood back to admire their handiwork. One classroom at the church had been transformed into a baby-themed extravaganza. Pastel-colored banners hung around the room along with cut out pictures of baby bottles, rattles, and pacifiers. On one wall, a piece of twine had been hung up to look like a clothesline and several pink and purple one-piece outfits were attached to it with clothespins.

Two long tables were covered with colorful tablecloths ready for people to sit down and visit. Another table held the snacks Mandy had prepared for the party, and a last table would hold all the gifts. A large box in colorful wrapping paper waited next to the table. Mandy and Raven had gone together and bought Tricia the stroller she had on the baby registry.

Raven brushed her hands off in front of her. "I say we outdid ourselves."

"I have to agree." Mandy smiled. "She'll love it. Oh, and can I say again how glad I am she didn't want to play a whole bunch of silly baby games?"

"Amen to that, sister." They both laughed.

Mandy moved to sit down. "I also think we were greatly overestimating how much time we needed to prepare for the party. It'll probably be at least thirty more minutes before anyone arrives."

"It'll give us plenty of time to talk about your hunky husband." The eye roll Mandy gave her didn't deter the line of questioning. "How are things going between you? Any more kissing?" Raven's eyes lit up in amusement.

Mandy thought about Preston. He'd dropped her off at the church before going to visit his parents. She'd text him when the party was over. "You seriously need a love life of your own. You know that, right?"

Raven stuck her bottom lip out in a fake pout. "I'd much rather live vicariously through you."

Mandy released an exaggerated sigh. "We're fine. There was more kissing. Things have felt a little different these last few days." She told Raven about the newest problems with the B&B. "Things are falling apart with the B&B, and I don't have a clue how to keep things together."

"Are you guys still keeping everything separate as far as financials go?"

"Yeah." Mandy frowned. "That's not what Preston wants to do, though. He'd be willing to bail the B&B out of trouble. But he's worked all his life for the opportunity to get his own business started. I don't want him sacrificing it for my mess and then we both end up with nothing to show for it."

"Did you tell him that?"

"Not in so many words." She was sure he understood her feelings on the matter. Fairly sure. Maybe. She suppressed a groan. "I don't see any other way around it. I can't let the B&B go. It's all I have left of Papa and Granny. And I can't let Preston lose everything he's worked for. So, I have to hope and pray something happens soon to turn things around."

Footsteps sounded from the hallway and Tricia walked in. The peach-colored dress she wore reached her calves and draped prettily over her extended belly.

The friends all hugged each other as Tricia gushed over the room. "You girls did a beautiful job! I love it!"

Mandy still couldn't believe her friend was going to be a mom. Tricia was one of the sweetest people Mandy had ever met. And the saying about pregnant women glowing? Tricia was the definition of that.

Tricia and her husband couldn't wait to meet their baby girl. It often made Mandy wonder if her parents were ever as excited to meet her. Did they get tired of being parents later? Or did their disappointment in parenthood start while Mandy was still in the womb?

This internal line of questioning was quickly putting a damper on Mandy's spirits. Besides, they were questions she'd never have the answer to. There was no doubt in her mind, though, that Tricia and her husband would be amazing parents.

Guests poured in and before long, the room was bustling. Everyone sampled the treats Mandy brought, and she had the satisfaction of seeing most of them disappear. When it came time to open gifts, Mandy wrote down each item and who had given it to Tricia. They received everything from adorable frilly outfits to a baby bathtub to a diaper bag.

By the time the last guest left, and they'd helped Tricia and her husband, Lars, load up the gifts, and Mandy and Raven had finished cleaning the room up again, Mandy was exhausted. At the same time, she hadn't thought about the B&B once in the last two hours. The tension seeped back into her body moments after remembering the trouble waiting for her back home. She fought against it, unwilling to stress yet.

Mandy texted Preston to let him know they were nearly done. She and Raven carried the two full trash bags out to the dumpster and walked around to the front of the church just in time to see Preston's truck enter the parking lot.

"That was fun." Raven reached over to give Mandy a hug. "So, who do you think will be the next one to have a baby?"

Mandy quirked an eyebrow. "My guess? Tricia again." They both laughed. "I had a blast. I'll call you soon, okay?"

Preston parked in a spot nearby and gave them a friendly wave.

"Sounds good." She nodded toward Preston. "You guys will figure things out."

"I know. Thanks, Raven." Mandy gave her friend a hug.

"You're welcome. When in doubt, kiss the man. That's bound to help at least a little." She waggled her eyebrows suggestively and giggled at herself.

"Uh-huh. Good bye, Raven." Mandy walked around the truck and climbed into the passenger seat. She set the small bag of dishware and a few leftovers from the party on the floorboard. "Hey. How was your visit with your parents?" She squinted against the sun shining through the windshield.

Preston took a pair of sunglasses out of the console and put them on. "It was good. Dad's got another cold, which worries me. He says it's not a big deal, but since the kidney transplant, it can get serious fast."

"Is your mom concerned, too?"

"Yeah, though we're both trying to not let Dad know." He chuckled wryly. "It'd stress him out and make it worse. But I asked her to call me if he gets any worse."

"I sure hope he's feeling better soon." Mandy took in the thick, fluffy clouds blanketing the sky in one direction, wondering if it might rain.

"Did Tricia enjoy her baby shower?"

The memory of Tricia laughing among friends and family members brought a smile to Mandy's face. "She did. It went off without a hitch. I swear Raven and I were the only ones without kids there. The one thing we did instead of games was to have a notebook where every guest wrote down a piece of advice for the new parents. Mine? 'Don't call me, I have no idea.'"

Preston laughed heartily at that. "I wouldn't be much better myself. With no siblings and no cousins in the area, I haven't had a lot of practice with babies." He remained quiet for a moment. "I know the kind of situation you grew up in, but did you ever hope to have a family of your own?"

Mandy couldn't have been more surprised by the question. At first, she didn't know how to answer it. She watched Preston's profile as he stared straight ahead. What kind of answer did he want? Had he hoped for a houseful of kids some day? If so, being married to her was pretty much putting a stop to that dream. A pang of guilt hit her, and she swallowed. "I thought about it a couple of times. I always figured it was safer to avoid the whole issue. I'd rather do that than risk repeating the past."

His head turned, and even with the sunglasses on, there was no missing the serious look on his face. "You are nothing like your parents, Mandy. If there's one thing I'm one hundred percent sure of in this life, that's it."

Those words immediately brought tears to her eyes. Granny had said as much several times before. But to hear it from Preston—She took a steadying breath and blinked them away. "Thanks," she whispered. She should probably ask him the same question. At least that's what was expected in polite conversation like this, but she couldn't quite bring herself to do it.

Preston must've sensed her unease, because he answered it anyway. "I'd like to have two or three kids." They stopped at a red light and he reached over for her hand. "But you are enough for me, Mandy. Don't ever doubt that."

He spoke the truth, of that she was sure. But it didn't help alleviate the guilt she alone stood between him and the dream he had for a family.

Chapter Sixteen

Preston opened the back door and found Mandy sitting in one of the wicker chairs. Rain pelted the porch roof and brought some much-needed moisture to the grass and plants. Best of all, the hot air had cooled and smelled clean. He took in a lungful as the screen door closed behind him. He motioned to the chair near Mandy. "Mind if I join you?"

"Of course not." She lifted her legs and tucked them under her. "I had to come out here for a while. I've been hoping it'd rain, although I'm glad it waited until after Tricia's baby shower." She watched the rain fall until a grin slowly lit up her face. "Do you remember when Papa sent us out to gather wood for a bonfire?"

Preston chuckled. "Yep. We wandered so far away that when it rained, we didn't have a prayer of getting the wood back before it got soaked. We had to dump it all and make a run for it."

"Which was pointless, considering we were already soaked to the bone."

It'd been funny even then. And Mandy, all of twelve years old and a skinny little thing, had looked like a drowned mouse. She shook like a leaf by the time they got back to the house. Mrs. Hudson met them at the door with warm towels and later, a cup of hot chocolate.

Things were much simpler back then.

"I've been thinking." Mandy's voice brought Preston out of his reverie. "Trying to keep the B&B is a losing battle. I realized that before, but I guess I didn't want to admit it." She frowned. "It's time to cut my losses. I'll let Jade and Elise go tomorrow, cancel the few remaining reservations we have, and focus on the web stuff." She turned her head to look at him. "What do you think?"

That she was asking for his opinion was big. She said nothing he hadn't thought through himself, but he'd hesitated to suggest such a big change. "I know that was a hard decision to make, but I agree that it's a wise one." He smiled at her. "You're talented. The website for Yarrow Woodworking looks awesome. Did you see the sales from today?" She shook her head. He moved his chair closer to her, took his phone out of his pocket, and showed her the numbers.

Her eyes widened. "Wow, this is amazing. You're turning the business into a success."

"No. *We* are. I couldn't have done it without your help. Without your grandfather's help." Would he ever convince her that Yarrow Woodworking was a family business—*their* family business? He watched as the rain collecting on the roof above them cascaded over the side like a small-scale waterfall. An idea came to him and he grinned. "You want to go out in the rain?"

"What? I don't think so." She crossed her arms

in front of herself and shook her head. But it was the hint of humor in her eyes that made Preston stand, put his phone on the chair, and hold a hand out to her.

"Come on. For old time's sake."

She looked like she'd object, but a smile lit up her face. She finally stood, set her phone down, and reached for his hand. "You're crazy, you know that?"

"Yep." *Crazy for you.* "I'm perfectly fine with it." He tugged her out from under the protective covering of the porch and into the cool rain. It'd slowed down a little, but it didn't take long before his skin was wet.

Mandy giggled as she shivered once and hunched her shoulders. "Now that'll wake you up. That's some cold rain." She lifted her chin, closed her eyes, and let the rain fall on her face.

Preston watched her, memorizing the way she looked with no visible cares in the world as she simply enjoyed the moment. When she opened her eyes again, he stepped forward and cupped her face with his hands. "You, Mandy Yarrow, are the most beautiful woman I've ever seen." Before she had the chance to speak, he covered her lips with his, caressing them with all the love he had to offer.

The rain fell harder, and the drops almost stung as they hit skin. Preston and Mandy broke the kiss at the same time and ran for the porch.

He shivered. "Okay, I'll admit it, you're right. That rain is cold."

"Told you." She tossed him a saucy look.

He wasn't about to let that one slide. He put his arms around her again and held her close. Just when she relaxed in his arms, he let his fingers dance along her ribs.

Mandy squealed and tried to squirm out of reach

as he tickled her. It only lasted a few moments, but by the time he stopped, they were both out of breath from laughing. She smacked him playfully on the arm and stepped back. "Not fair."

"Maybe not, but it was fun."

~*~

It was late Monday morning and Mandy was already exhausted. Talking to Jade and Elise and telling them she wouldn't need their services anymore was hard enough, but then she had to cancel the two remaining reservations. Thankfully, both people were understanding and even thanked her for the hotel referrals.

The Hudson Bed and Breakfast was no more.

She had a lot of guilt about putting an end to the business Papa and Granny had built up for so many years. Would they have been disappointed in her inability to keep it running if they could see it now? At the same time, things had gotten so bad and stressful, there was a measure of relief knowing she wouldn't be fighting to keep it continuing when all odds were against it. Goodness knew she'd tried almost everything she could think of.

It was one thing to drag the B&B down. But Preston had given up a lot to marry Mandy. She didn't want anything to jeopardize the business he was building. While the B&B had been struggling financially, Yarrow Woodworking had seen more success than either of them hoped for. Mandy couldn't be happier for Preston. He deserved this.

Hopefully she could get a few more web clients and make enough to continue paying for the second mortgage Papa had taken take out a few years ago, much less the other bills. If things would stabilize…

She tried to distract herself by focusing on her laptop and making some headway with work. Twenty minutes later, she gave up and headed upstairs. Ever since Granny's passing, Mandy had avoided going into her room. She'd even let Elise be the one to dust and water the plants Granny loved. But today, something drew her into the room. Maybe it was a need to be near Granny, she didn't know. Instead of the overwhelming pain of grief, crossing the threshold also brought a level of peace.

Everything in the room spoke of Granny. The faint lilac smell of her favorite perfume. The macramé plant hangers on either side of the large window. Granny once told Mandy she made those back in her creative years. Even the photo of her and Papa that rested on the table by the bed brought a smile to Mandy's face.

She went farther into the room and reached up to finger the delicate leaves of the fern growing from a pot in one hanger. Most of the fronds grew on the side of the pot closest to the window, but a few reached as far as the wall and had climbed over the curtain rod.

The other pot and hanger held a spider plant. The spiderlings, which could be clipped and soaked to create a new plant, flourished.

"I miss you, Granny. It's not the same here without you."

Her own voice sounded loud in the silence of the room. She wandered to the dresser and opened the wooden jewelry box. The top lifted to reveal spaces for rings and bracelets. Below that, two drawers held everything else.

As a girl, Mandy would sit on the bed and go through the jewelry box with Granny. Mandy would admire the pretty rings, shiny bracelets, and dainty earrings. Granny always let her try some of them on and said she'd give them all to her one day.

The silver ring with a turquoise flower stood out among the rest. It'd always been one of Mandy's favorites. Tentatively, she lifted it from its resting place and slipped it onto the ring finger of her right hand. It fit perfectly. She decided she would wear the ring always in memory of her grandparents.

She perused the jewelry, and Granny's voice whispered from memory as she told Mandy how she'd gotten each piece.

The floor creaked from the doorway, and Mandy turned to find Preston watching her. He looked uncertain. "I wanted to see if you were ready for lunch. I'm sorry if I interrupted."

"No, it's fine." Mandy carefully closed the lid of the jewelry box. "I figured it was time to travel down memory lane a little." She shrugged. "Lunch sounds great. I'll be right there."

"Okay." He gave her an understanding smile.

She took in the peace of the room one more time before retrieving the picture of her grandparents. She placed it on the side table in her room next to the picture of her and Preston before going downstairs to find him.

He noticed the turquoise ring on her right hand and pointed to it. "That's really pretty."

"Thanks." She smiled as she looked at the dainty flower. "Papa gave it to Granny on their second anniversary. I can't remember where he bought it, but Granny wore this ring for years until it no longer fit.

It's always been one of my favorites."

"It looks good on your hand. I'm sure your grandparents would like that you're wearing it."

"I think so, too." She took a bite of her reheated fried chicken. "How's work going?"

"Really well. The circular saw was giving me trouble, but I got it to see things my way." He winked at her.

"I'll bet you did. You're pretty persistent." The corners of Mandy's mouth lifted with mischief.

"Funny." He leaned back in his chair and pierced her with a mock serious glare, humor glittering in his eyes. "You've got a more than healthy dose of persistence yourself, missy."

She shrugged and focused on her chicken, but she couldn't keep her smile from growing. "I have no idea what you're talking about."

That night, Mandy yawned as she crawled into bed, welcoming the smooth, cool sheets against her skin. It would be nice not having to worry about guests anymore. She'd been helping Granny and Jade make huge breakfasts for years. The idea of waking up and eating a bowl of cereal sounded like a vacation.

Mandy wasn't sure how long she'd been asleep when there was a knock on her bedroom door. It sounded again before she woke up enough to sit up in bed and blink at the darkness. "Preston?"

The door opened a little. "Hey, sorry to wake you. My mom just called and they took Dad by ambulance to the hospital. He's having trouble breathing and Mom couldn't get him into the car."

She jumped out of bed and pulled the door open the rest of the way. "Oh, no!"

The light from Preston's room and the bathroom filled the hallway and spilled through the doorway. He was dressed although his hair still looked mussed from sleep and he didn't have shoes or socks on yet. His eyes brimmed with worry. "I'm going to drive in and check on them."

"Of course." Mandy flipped her light on. "If you'll give me a minute to get dressed, I'll come with you."

"Are you sure? You don't have to. It's two in the morning."

"Absolutely."

Relief replaced some of the concern on his face. "Thanks. I'll meet you downstairs?"

"I'll be quick."

He nodded and left, closing the door behind him.

Twenty minutes later, they pulled into the hospital parking lot and found a spot as close to the emergency room as they could. Mandy flinched as frigid air hit them when they went through the revolving doors. She reached for Preston's hand. *Please, God. Watch over Stanley and guide the hands of the doctors. Help him to be okay.*

They checked with admissions and were directed to one of the ER rooms. Once there, they found Ellen pacing the room, her hands clasped in front of her. The moment she saw them, she embraced them both. "Oh, I'm glad you two are here."

"Where's Dad?"

"They took him down for an X-ray. They think he's got pneumonia." Ellen held onto Preston's arm. "The last time this happened, he was in the hospital for a week."

Mandy had done a little reading about kidney transplants and the dangers that could arise in the weeks and years afterward. She understood getting sick might be worse for Stanley than someone who had a stronger immune system. She reached out and rubbed Ellen's back. "We're praying for him. Hopefully it won't be as bad this time."

"I hope you're right." Ellen's chin quivered, and she gave Mandy another hug.

They waited until a nurse brought Stanley back into the room. He was already on an IV and they got him set up with a nose cannula to give him some extra oxygen. "Someone will be with you as soon as the doctor goes over those X-rays."

Stanley gave her a half wave. The bright eyes and smile Mandy was used to seeing were missing from his face. He looked at her and for a moment, Mandy was worried he might not want her to be there. After all, it was bad enough being sick without having extra people in the room. She was seconds away from saying something about how she could go to the waiting room when he reached a hand out to her. "Thank you for coming."

"Of course." She took his hand, and he gave it a squeeze before releasing it again.

As she watched Preston interact with his parents, she wondered what it would've been like to have caring parents of her own. Would she be visiting them for dinner nearly every week? Would they be happy if she came to help out at the hospital?

And then a thought hit her hard enough to take her breath. She'd *had* that with her grandparents. Maybe their titles were different, but the love and care they showed her wasn't. A smile lifted one corner of her mouth. She couldn't have asked for better parents than Papa and Granny. They'd stood in the gap for her and made a difference in her life. A huge one at that.

"You okay?" Preston's voice was low and right next to her ear.

"I am." His arm came around her, and she leaned into him, absorbing his warmth.

Two hours later, the doctor informed them Stanley had a touch of pneumonia, but it looked like they had caught it early. They wanted to keep Stanley overnight, and if he responded well to the breathing treatments, might even send him home by tomorrow evening.

Ellen's face lit up as she looked at her husband. She leaned over and gave him a gentle kiss before turning her attention to the doctor. "Wonderful. Thank you so much!"

Mandy saw Preston visibly relax as his shoulders lowered a little, and he smiled. "Great news, Dad. Remember not to push yourself. If you don't feel well enough to go home, you tell them."

"I will, son."

Ellen turned toward Preston and Mandy. "You two go on home and get some sleep. I'll call you if anything changes. There's no sense in you sitting around here."

"You sure, Mom?" Preston reached for her and gave her a hug.

"Absolutely." She hugged Mandy, too. "Thank you both. We sure appreciate you."

A few minutes later, they were on their way out of the hospital and back to the truck in the parking lot. It was after five in the morning, and the sun would be up soon.

Mandy hadn't felt tired the whole time they were at the hospital, but now a yawn claimed her as she settled into the seat.

"Sleepy?"

"A little," she admitted. "You?"

"Yeah. I'll be better once Dad's home, but I'm relieved it wasn't any worse." He gave her a little smile. "Thanks for coming with me tonight. It meant a lot to have you there." His eyes revealed his sincerity.

"Of course. Your parents are great and I'm glad your dad's going to be okay." Mandy placed her hand on his arm. "Your parents are lucky to have you for a son. I…I'm lucky to have you in my life, too."

His face transformed into a grin. "Right back at ya." He put the keys in the ignition and started the engine. "What do you say we go home?"

"I think that sounds like a great idea." She yawned again and settled into her seat. *Thank you, God, for watching over Stanley tonight. Please continue to help him improve.* She glanced at Preston's profile. *Thanks for bringing Preston into my life. I don't know what I would've done all these years without his friendship. I guess You knew exactly what I needed, didn't You?*

Chapter Seventeen

Mandy finished scrubbing the potatoes in the sink and had just turned the water off when Preston came in through the back door. "Hey," she said over her shoulder. "I need to get this going before I can take a break for lunch."

"It smells good in here. What are you making?" Preston peeked into the frying pan on the stove where beef was simmering.

"Stew. My friend Tricia texted me, and she went into early labor. They have her on bed rest. Everything's okay, but I decided to make a big batch of stew and take it to her this afternoon. We can take some to your parents' this evening, too. Have you heard from them? Is Stanley still going home today?"

He turned and leaned against the counter. "Yes, hopefully they'll discharge him before too long. They're waiting for the doctor to make his rounds and check on Dad one more time." He nodded toward the potatoes. "That's a sweet thing to do. Can I help?"

His offer surprised her. "You don't have to. It

shouldn't take me too long."

"I don't mind." Preston washed his hands in the other sink basin. "Tell me what you want me to do."

Mandy used to spend her time in the kitchen visiting with Granny. She hadn't realized how lonely she was, working on her own. "If you'll cut these potatoes, I'll do the same with the carrots and onions."

"Sounds like a plan." He went to the knife block and withdrew the largest blade. "This should do the trick."

She chuckled. "I'd sure like to think so."

They worked in tandem to fill the pot with chopped vegetables. They chatted about the lack of sleep, how hard it would be for Stanley to make himself rest for awhile, and how Papa had been just as bad anytime he was sick.

When they finished with the vegetables, Mandy poured broth into the pot, added the beef, and set the whole thing on the stove to heat up.

"I don't suppose there'll be enough of that for us to eat tonight, too, will there?" The hopeful look on Preston's face made Mandy smile.

"There'll be plenty. I'm planning on making a pan of cornbread to go with it."

His eyebrows rose and a playful glint lit up his eyes. "Have I mentioned you're my favorite wife?"

That made her laugh. "I'm glad you approve. I thought about making brownies, but I wasn't sure whether your dad could have sweets or not. Do you know?"

"I don't." Preston wiped his hands off on a towel and stood in front of her. He leaned forward and kissed her briefly on the lips. "But I can have them." He winked.

"Well, you did help me make dinner. It only seems fair." Mandy realized that not only was Preston flirting with her, but she was dishing it right back. Flirtation was never something she was comfortable with, but this was easy. Natural. When had that happened?

"I like the way you think." He kissed her again. "And if Dad gets the go ahead, maybe I'll share a brownie or two with him." He paused. "Can I come with you?"

"Where?"

"To take stew over to Lars and Tricia's. I'd like to go with you."

Boy, he was full of surprises today. "Are you sure you can get away?"

"I made a lot of progress this morning. I think it'd do me good to take the afternoon off. Do you mind?"

His thoughtfulness warmed her heart. "I'd like that. We can head over there about two. That way we can visit for a few minutes and not tire her out too much."

"Sounds perfect."

~*~

Mandy gave Tricia a hug before introducing Preston and Lars. The men shook hands and visited about work. Mandy carefully sat down next to her friend on the couch.

Tricia laughed. "I'm not going to break. The doctor mainly said I need to stay off my feet."

"I can't believe this. You were fine for the baby shower. We didn't tire you out too much, did we?"

"No." Tricia rubbed her large baby bump and gave it a pat. "This little one is in a hurry to meet her mommy and daddy. We're hoping we can get her to stay put for another couple of weeks. I'll be thirty-seven weeks along then, and my doctor said they'll let things progress at that point."

Two weeks. At least this hadn't happened earlier. One lady from church had gone into pre-term labor at twenty-two weeks and spent months in the hospital. "So, what are you going to do for fourteen days?"

Lars spoke up, his eyebrows raised for emphasis. "She'll stay off her feet and let her husband help her. I had extra vacation saved up, so I took one week off, and then Tricia's mom is flying in for the second week." He gave Preston a look that insinuated he'd know what it was like to have a persistent wife. "If we don't have someone here with her, Tricia will be up cleaning or something anyway."

"That's not true!" Tricia scowled at her husband but couldn't keep the serious face for long. "I stay off my feet."

Lars shook his head at Preston who chuckled.

"Oh!" Tricia shifted her hand a little. "See, Jasmine says you need to be nice to her mama."

Mandy watched as Tricia's whole belly shifted to one side a little and bounced back again. She'd felt Jasmine move twice when Tricia insisted she put her hand over the kicks, but it was insane to watch this. She tried to picture the baby all curled up in there. What would it be like to carry a baby for nine months and wonder what he or she looked like? She imagined the doctor handing a little bundle to her as she and Preston counted ten fingers and ten toes—

She shook herself when she realized what was

going through her head. The others were talking, and she looked up to find Preston watching her with concern and something else she didn't recognize. Her face warmed, and she stood suddenly. "You know what? I'm going to find a place for the stew in your fridge. I'll be right back."

Once in the kitchen, Mandy leaned against the counter and rolled her eyes. What had gotten into her? She'd never imagined having a baby before. Obviously, between hanging out with Tricia and the shower last weekend, it was the baby overload that was causing her wandering thoughts. That and the lack of sleep last night. Having rationalized it, she shifted things around in Tricia's fridge and put the stew on one shelf. When she turned around, she found Preston standing in the doorway.

"You need any help?"

"No, I've got it. And it's fine for the cornbread and brownies to sit out until they're ready to eat." She moved to walk past him, but he stopped her by pulling her into his arms.

"You are a kind and thoughtful person, Mandy. Your parents have no idea what they missed out on when they chose not to be in your life." He pressed a kiss to her forehead. "I can't imagine mine without you in it."

Mandy squeezed her eyes shut and welcomed the warmth of his arms. It ended way too quickly when he stepped back, put an arm around her shoulders, and walked with her back into the living room.

As Preston worked on Friday, he smiled to

himself and thought things might finally be turning around. Sales had continued to increase every day. Mr. Logan brought in more items on consignment than Preston had dared to hope. Time would tell how much of it the tourists would purchase. Not only that, but Dad was on the mend and the weather had finally cooled. They'd be enjoying temperatures in the seventies for the foreseeable future.

Mandy had been spending hours upon hours working on the different websites she managed. Even though he said nothing to her about it, Preston worried she was overworking herself. But if all went the way he hoped it would, sooner than later they'd have enough money coming in to allow the B&B to become more of a hobby or supplemental income. That was the goal, anyway. At least no one else had been harassing her about selling the place. It was a good thing, too, because he'd been ready to march down to Vincent's place and have a word.

Best of all? It was becoming clear his beautiful wife was changing toward him. He'd been able to steal several kisses, and she'd been flirting with him. Mandy. He wouldn't have believed it if he hadn't seen it with his own eyes. And yes, he was enjoying every minute of it. Spending more than a month married to Mandy only convinced him even further how right they were together. He prayed every day that she'd see that, too.

After lunch, Preston whistled as he made his way from the house to the workshop. The sky was shrouded in thick clouds hinting at rain in the future. Just before four that afternoon, a clap of thunder shook the workshop. Preston set the sander down and checked the weather on his phone. They were under a severe thunderstorm warning for the next half hour with heavy rain and large hail expected. In addition, there was a tornado watch in effect. That meant the conditions could lead to one, and it was best to stay alert just in case. Not an unusual weather forecast this time of the year. But Preston decided he'd rather be at the house with Mandy during the storm and called his workday good.

It was already raining when he exited the workshop. By the time he reached the back porch, it had turned into a downpour. Mandy met him at the door, holding it open for him. Once inside, he turned to marvel at the rain, which made it hard to even see the workshop.

Mandy rubbed her arms and the goosebumps that covered her skin. "We needed rain, but this is crazy."

Preston would've put his arms around her to warm her up except it might make it worse, as wet as he was. He was just about to go in and grab a towel when the first *thunk* hit the roof over the porch. That was followed by two and then three more. Within seconds, marble-sized hail pummeled the ground and bounced off the edges of the porch.

"I haven't seen hail like this in a long time." Preston watched as the ground started to look more white than green. A louder thud hit the roof, and a piece of hail the size of a small plum landed on the porch and rolled to Mandy's feet. "Come on, we need to get inside."

He hadn't finished his sentence before both of them were scrambling to get indoors. More of the larger hail began to fall, and the sound was deafening.

"This is some of the largest hail I've ever seen." Mandy had to raise her voice to be heard over the noise.

"Yeah, me, too."

Suddenly, a loud crack resounded from the living room followed by the shattering of glass. They ran into the room to see hail had hit one of the windows. Glass littered the floor below it. At least it sounded like the hail was beginning to subside.

"I'll go get the broom and dust pan." There was no missing the resignation in Mandy's voice.

When she returned, Preston took them from her. "Hey, this isn't a big deal. I've put windows in myself before. I'll go get some new glass and have it installed tomorrow."

"You don't think I should call the insurance company?"

"We'll take a look around outside when the storm ends. If the window is the only thing that's been damaged, the deductible will be more than the repairs. No sense in worrying about it until we know more."

She nodded her agreement. They worked together to clean up the mess and then Preston changed into some dry clothes. After making soup and grilled cheese sandwiches, they sat down in the living room and watched the weather channel while they ate. The sun was setting by the time the storm cleared enough for them to go outside.

Preston wasn't sure what he expected to see when they stepped onto the front porch. Mandy's gasp drew his attention to the flower beds along the front of the house. The hail had ripped through them like paper. Flower petals were scattered over the ground and at least two of the bushes probably wouldn't recover at all.

Mandy's chin quivered. "I can't believe most of

Granny's flowers are gone. She'd be devastated."

He put his arms around her. "It's been one thing after another. It's okay to be upset, Mandy. Even to cry."

"No." Mandy pushed away from him and steeled her jaw. "They're just flowers, right? They'll grow back, or we'll plant more in the spring."

Preston used one finger to gather some of the loose strands of hair framing her face and swept them behind her ear. "I'm proud of you, do you know that?" She shrugged, and he kissed her briefly. "Come on, let's see how everything else looks."

When all was said and done, damage to the house was minimal. The broken window and the plants had taken the worst of it. They decided it wasn't worth contacting house insurance and dealing with the deductible.

The cars, on the other hand, had a different story. Both had multiple large dents on the hood and roof. "We are going to have to call insurance for this, though." Preston was glad they'd combined policies.

"Wow, they took a beating." Mandy ran a hand over the hood of her car. "I'll go in and see where I can dig up the funds for the deductible."

Preston suppressed a sigh. The woman's stubborn streak ran a mile long. "We've got the money in the woodworking bank account. We'll pay for it out of there." He was prepared for an argument. He expected her to at least insist on paying half of the deductible herself.

She finally gave a small nod. "Okay." She turned to look at him. "I think that sounds like a plan."

"Good." He put his arm around her and steered them back toward the house. He'd been ready for another battle over where the money would come from and this was a pleasant surprise. "Let's go call and file claims on the cars. We'll come out here tomorrow and get all of this cleaned up."

~*~

Mandy handed Preston another long piece of tape. He used it to secure a thick section of cardboard over the jagged hole in the window. It was nearly eleven at night. Between the sun going down and the rain earlier, the temperature had cooled off drastically. Mandy was almost cold and looked forward to changing into something warmer before bed.

Preston tapped the window. "We're not supposed to get any more storms. This should hold until I can get a new window pane put in tomorrow. Do you want to come with me to the home improvement store?"

"Yeah, I'd like that."

"Good." He smiled. "We can look at the garden department, too, though we probably want to wait until spring to plant anything new."

He was right. While it still looked like their first freeze was weeks away, you just never knew what to expect from the weather in Texas—aside from the fact it was unpredictable.

"I've always liked Texas sage. Those would look pretty along the front of the house. Maybe we can just re-do the flower beds. I don't think Papa would mind."

"I don't think he would, either. Besides, we can do it together." He turned to face her, a twinkle in his eyes. "If you haven't noticed, I rather enjoy spending time with you." There was that wink of his again.

Mandy's pulse jumped. "I do, too. With you, I mean." She suppressed an eyeroll at herself. She really should just stop talking now.

Preston chuckled and took a step closer, his shoes touching the tips of her toes. He fingered a section of her hair. "The last month hasn't been easy for either of us. There's been a lot of adjustment. I want you to know I appreciate everything you've been doing."

"I appreciate everything you've done, too." She swallowed her nerves. "Can I admit something?" He motioned for her to continue. "This...us...hasn't been as hard as I thought it'd be." It was true. She still wasn't so sure what their future together looked like. The fear and uncertainty that had bubbled up in the beginning gave way to curiosity and hope. In fact, she found it more and more difficult to keep the distance between herself and Preston than she'd originally sworn she would.

His hands held hers and then slowly moved up her arms. He gazed into her eyes before focusing on her lips. "Mandy..."

He kissed her then, his arms wrapping around her like a warm cocoon of safety and promises. Mandy melted into his embrace as he deepened the kiss.

Minutes later, he put his forehead to hers, and they both took shaky breaths. He ran the back of his hand down her cheek. "I don't want to be alone tonight. Do you?"

It was the last thing Mandy wanted right now, either. She shook her head.

Preston's eyes closed for a moment before he softly kissed the tip of her nose. He took her hand in his and they headed upstairs together.

Chapter Eighteen

Preston awoke trying to sort through his dream and reality. The moment he felt Mandy's sleeping form beside him, he smiled. This was what he'd wanted for longer than he could remember: To wake up next to the woman he loved every day for the rest of his life.

He breathed in, expecting her familiar scent to fill his nose. When he inhaled something acrid instead, he lurched upright in bed. That's when he noticed the high-pitched beeping downstairs and realized what had awakened him in the first place.

The alarms upstairs chimed in and Mandy sat with a start. "Preston?"

"There's smoke. We've got to get out of here and call the fire department."

He grabbed his phone and wallet off the side table and shoved it into the pocket of his knit shorts. Then he snagged a T-shirt off the chair and pulled it on. Mandy came around the bed, her fear-brimmed eyes focused on his, and reached for his hand.

The darkened hallway greeted them. Mandy's

hand slipped from Preston's as she dashed into her room. "Mandy!" She returned to the doorway in moments with the framed photograph of her grandparents, the other from their wedding, and her phone. He shoved her phone into one of his pockets and reclaimed her hand. He had no intention of letting her get away from him again.

The smoke became stronger as they descended the stairs. Preston tamped down his alarm at the eerie orange glow emanating from the kitchen area. It caused strange shadows of the dining room table and chairs that seemed to dance against the walls. Mandy coughed then pulled the front of her shirt up to cover her face.

He led her through the living room and out the front door. Once they got a little distance from the house, Preston dialed 911. "I need to report a house fire." He gave them the address. As he spoke, he picked his way across the grass in his bare feet to the side of the house. From there, they saw the back porch was consumed in flames. "Yes, the fire seems to be originating from the kitchen. I understand. We'll stay outside." He hung up the call and glanced at Mandy. She stared at the house as though she couldn't quite process what was happening. He tightened his hold on her hand. "The fire department is on the way."

"I can't believe this is happening."

"I know." He dropped her hand and instead put his arms around her waist. She let her back relax against his chest. "Me, neither." It was only then he realized they were in bare feet. All the rain from the night before had turned the ground soggy. Water and mud seeped through the grass beneath the soles of his feet.

They stood in silence and watched as the orange and yellow flames continued to make their mark on the beautiful house. Even when the fire department arrived and fought the fire, Mandy remained silent. Men worked together to douse the persistent flames. The stench of the smoke was all Preston could smell now. After what seemed like an eternity, the flames died down. The floodlights from the fire engine revealed a charred hole where the back of the house used to be. The porch was nothing but a skeleton now and looked like it would collapse with the slightest breeze.

The sun began to peek its head up over the horizon, the orange glow of the sky almost an echo of what had consumed a portion of the house. How much damage had been done? Was anything recoverable? After everything Mandy had endured over the last month, Preston worried this would be more than she could take.

She trembled against him and dropped the framed photograph of her grandparents. It hit the ground at her feet with a crack. When she bent to turn it over, the glass from the front was now only shards on the grass. At least that had protected the image itself from getting wet. Her chin dipped and rested against her chest as her shoulders fell.

One man from the fire department approached. Mandy stood again, clutching what was left of the picture frame in both hands.

Preston shook the man's hand. "Thanks so much for your quick work."

Soot marred the fireman's face. "We got the flames out as fast as we could. It'll be some time before you can go inside and see what all has been damaged. Unfortunately, the kitchen was gutted and the two bedrooms upstairs on that side have been destroyed."

Mandy and Mrs. Hudson's bedrooms. Mandy sagged against Preston, and he put an arm around her waist to support her.

He swallowed. "What about the rest of the house?"

"There will be smoke and water damage. Hopefully you'll be able to salvage a good amount from the rest. But this house isn't livable. You'll have to contact your insurance company and have an adjuster determine whether it can be repaired or not." The guy didn't look real positive about that last bit.

Looking at the house now, Preston doubted it himself. "Any idea what caused the fire?"

"We're going to have to do some further investigation. It looks like it may have been some old wiring behind the stove." He turned and motioned to one of the other firemen who stood nearby.

"This is an older house. Do you know when the wiring was last inspected?"

Mandy shook her head. "No. I have no idea." She said nothing else as the firemen told them what they could expect over the next few days. When they left again, Preston turned his attention to her.

She still wore the shorts and oversized shirt she'd been sleeping in. He looked down at the impressions their bare feet had made in the grass. They needed somewhere to stay and some clothes. "Are you cold, Mandy?"

"No. At least, I don't think so." She'd been clutching the photo frame to her chest and lowered it. That's when they both noticed one of her hands had blood on it. She stretched her palm out, revealing a small cut by her thumb. "Probably from the broken glass." Her head lifted, and she looked at the front of the house. "I guess we'll have enough damage to report the broken window after all." She tried to smile, but it didn't quite reach her eyes.

Wordlessly, Preston took her hand and led her over to his truck. He helped her sit down on the passenger seat, still facing the door. He reached around her and retrieved a tissue from the console and pressed it to the cut on her hand. If they hadn't smelled the smoke when they did, or gotten out of the house fast enough to call the fire department... Preston swallowed hard. He could've lost her.

What was going to happen if the house couldn't be repaired? This place meant too much to Mandy. It was the only reason she'd agreed to the marriage in the first place. Without the B&B, would she want the marriage dissolved? She said she'd never get a divorce. But would that change if she no longer had all of this to fall back on? After all the time they'd spent together the last couple of weeks, and last night in particular, he didn't think so. He wanted to push those concerns out, but they refused to release their hold on him.

Mandy stared at the tissue on her hand as red seeped through the layers. She couldn't feel the pain from the cut. Preston had asked if she was cold. She wasn't. Truthfully, she felt nothing right now. Everything was muted. Numb.

She looked at the house. From the front, you wouldn't know what kind of damage the place had sustained. Many of her personal things had been in her room. Destroyed. And Granny and Papa's stuff...

Preston gently placed a hand under her chin and

lifted her gaze to his. "I'm worried about you, Mandy."

She saw the truth of his statement in his eyes. "Everything's gone. Papa. Granny. Now the house. Gone." Tears filled her eyes and this time, instead of fighting against it, she let them flow. For the first time in longer than she could remember, Mandy cried. The salty streams carried with them the pain of being abandoned by her parents and the grief of her grandparents' death. Sobs racked her body as Preston held her close and spoke softly against her hair.

Knowing the only home she'd ever had was damaged—possibly beyond repair—meant the last connection to her grandparents might be lost forever.

The waves of grief crashed mercilessly against her heart. She tried to focus on the words Preston said and realized he was praying for her. Praying for peace and the comfort only God could give her, and thanking Him they both made it out of the fire safely. Only then did the pain she was experiencing ease just a little. The sound of his heartbeat filled her ears, slowly working to calm the frantic beating of her own.

Mandy hiccupped and drew in a slow breath. "What are we going to do, Preston?"

"The only thing we can do. Pray and take it one thing at a time."

It all seemed like a blur as Preston drove her to his parents' house. Ellen immediately drew Mandy to her in a hug. "I'm sorry this happened. It's absolutely terrible." She looked up at Preston. "I've got a call into the church and they are rounding up clothing donations to bring by later this morning. But for now," she gave Mandy a reassuring smile, "you two need to get cleaned up and get some rest. I can only imagine how exhausted you must be." She led the way to the spare room at the other end of the house. "They may not fit perfectly, but here are some clean clothes. If you need anything else, please let us know."

"This is great, Mom. Thank you." Preston kissed her cheek.

Ellen left and Mandy stood staring at the neatly folded clothes on the end of the bed. Maybe Ellen was right. Mandy was exhausted, making it impossible to think straight right now.

Preston picked up one stack and handed it to her. "You go get a shower first. Then come in here and get some sleep. I'll get cleaned up when you're done."

It wasn't until the warm water pelted her skin that she comprehended how much dirt and smoke she'd brought with her. She had to shampoo her hair three times to get the smoke smell out.

The warm water relaxed her muscles a little and by the time she turned the water off and got dressed in clean clothes, she was yawning. She'd had to remove the bandage from her hand and, since the cut stopped bleeding some time ago, didn't worry about leaving it exposed.

The sound of voices in the other room drifted down the hall as Mandy padded her way to the spare room. Preston had put her phone and both the photo frames she'd managed to get out of the house on the little table next to the bed. She lay down and tried to get comfortable. Her whole body ached and her eyes hurt from the smoke and all the crying. Yet, her mind refused to stop churning and allow her to fall asleep.

She was vaguely aware of the shower starting up in the bathroom. A while later, a creak in the floor brought Mandy's head up. She found Preston in the doorway, studying her. He walked forward, his face full of concern. "You okay? Why aren't you resting?"

Mandy shrugged. "I can't fall asleep." She pointed to the image of her grandparents. "I keep staring at their picture. They'd be devastated if they saw what happened to the house. Depending on how badly everything was damaged, this and my ring may be all I have of them." More tears silently escaped her eyes and flowed, dripping off her nose and cheek and onto the bedspread below her. How was it possible she had any tears left to cry?

"If there's anything I can do, you know I will."

She squeezed her eyes shut, stopping the flow of tears. He would do anything for her. He'd demonstrated that by marrying her to save the B&B. And for what? To have it destroyed weeks later? Her head pounded with the swirl of thoughts and emotions that refused to let up. She rolled over to face him, her head resting on the arm bent beneath it. "Will you hold me?"

Preston's eyes softened, and he set his stuff on the dresser nearby. "Of course." He lay down beside her, gathered her into his arms, and held her close.

Mandy released a shaky breath. It took only seconds of listening to the sound of his heartbeat for blessed sleep to finally claim her.

Preston watched in amazement as several members of the church carried bags and boxes into his parents' living room. Mandy reached for his hand. Her eyes were wide as she slowly shook her head, and he assumed she was as shocked as he was at the outpouring of love.

Mrs. Whipple gave Mandy a tight hug and then Mom as well. "Now, I brought enough food for lunch and dinner for you all today. Someone should be bringing a meal by every day for the next week so y'all don't have to cook."

"Thank you so much," Mandy said sincerely.

"Are you kidding? We'd do anything for Samantha and Barry's granddaughter. Don't think another thing of it." She patted Mandy's cheek.

Pastor Dan shook Preston's hand and then Dad's as well. "Go through the boxes and keep any clothing you can use. Whatever you don't want, just bring it by the church or call, and I'll come pick it up again."

"I appreciate it, sir. Mandy and I can't thank you enough for what you've done. All of you." He put an arm around Mandy's waist.

She nodded. "Thank you so much." Her voice broke.

Pastor Dan prayed for them and their situation. "Remember, if you need anything, let us know. We can organize a group of people to help clean up the place or make repairs. Or if you find you need more than what's in the boxes, we can figure something out."

They walked their visitors to the door and waved good bye.

"This is incredible." Mandy looked like she didn't know where to begin.

Ellen pointed to the boxes. "Why don't you kids start going through the clothing. We've got Wilma Whipple's famous chicken spaghetti for lunch. I'm going to toss the salad, and we can eat while we make a list of the other things you'll need."

Dad pushed himself up from his chair. "I'll help you out, honey. If I sit around much longer, my legs will forget what they're supposed to do." He laughed at his own joke.

Preston watched his parents go into the kitchen. Dad had improved a lot over the last few days, although Mom regularly reminded him to take it easy. He also had every intention of going back to work on Monday. He wasn't happy about the extra time off but admitted it'd be better to recover completely than to risk getting sick again.

Preston moved one of the boxes to the coffee table and turned to Mandy. "You doing okay?"

"Better than I probably should be. I'm not sure if that's a good thing or a bad thing." She pulled her hair back and twisted it into a bun. When she let go, it fell to cascade around her shoulders again.

He tucked a stray wisp behind one of her ears. "Everything's so messed up right now, I'm not sure, either." He kissed her and pulled her into a hug. "But God's doing a pretty amazing job of providing what we need so far." Mandy nodded against his chest. "There is one thing I'm going to miss once we go through these clothes and get everything organized."

"What's that?" She took a step back, her brow furrowed.

Preston grinned. "I like seeing you wear my old shirts Mom found in the closet."

She looked down at her oversize shirt and blushed furiously. "Yeah, well, don't get used to it." She reached for the box. Some of her hair fell forward to block her smile.

Chapter Nineteen

Late in the evening, two days later, they got the official word from the insurance company. It would cost a lot more than they could afford to repair the house, even with the insurance money. Mandy had known in her heart this was coming.

Preston looked at her in concern from his spot beside her on the Yarrow's couch. His parents were thoughtful enough to leave the room once the call had come in. "I was hoping we'd hear differently. I'm sorry, Mandy."

"Me, too." Even though she was disappointed, the pain she expected to experience at the news didn't cut nearly as deep as she thought it would.

"They'll have a company clean out the house and make sure we get everything that's salvageable. Since the fire was contained in one side of the house, I'm hoping that means not everything was lost."

"I wonder how long something like that takes?" She wiped the palms of her hands off on her jeans. She'd often visualized the house and tried to guess what might have made it through the fire. The most important things were in her bedroom and Granny's. But not everything. "I'm glad the workshop remained untouched." The little smile on her face fell as guilt bubbled up. "I'm sorry I haven't been able to go out there with you and help yet. I got some website work done earlier today, though. Tomorrow, I should be able to jump back into everything. I'll see about taking on some more clients, too."

Preston shook his head. "Don't rush, Mandy."

Mandy looked toward the door to the kitchen and lowered her voice. "Your parents have been absolutely amazing, but we can't stay here forever. I don't want them feeling crowded. If I can get caught up on the web work, and if the contractors will get back to you with some estimates soon..."

He didn't let her finish. "Please, give me until the end of the week. I promise you, we'll figure something out."

She wanted to object, but the near desperation in his eyes made her agree. "Okay." A yawn escaped, and she covered her mouth with one hand.

Preston stood when she did. "Don't give up, Mandy." He leaned over and brushed his lips against hers. "Let's tell my parents good night and get you to bed. You look like you're about ready to drop."

"I am tired." As Mandy readied for bed, she kept thinking about Preston. There was a difference in him that suggested he had something on his mind, but she couldn't quite put her finger on what. She wanted to question him, but she didn't even know what to ask.

They'd get some sleep tonight and tomorrow her head would be clearer.

~*~

Mandy woke the next morning. With her eyes still closed, she put a hand on the other side of the bed, expecting to find Preston there, still sleeping. When all she felt were blankets, she opened her eyes. The early morning light filtered through the curtains in front of the windows. Where the curtains parted, a thin stream of light made its way through and lit up the photograph of Papa and Granny. Next to it on the table was a wrapped gift with a card on top and her name written on the envelope in Preston's handwriting. When had he left it here? She must have been sleeping hard if she hadn't even heard him get ready and leave this morning.

Curious, she reached for the gift and set it on her lap. She withdrew the card and read the note written inside.

Mandy,

You are the most important person in my life. When we got married, I promised I'd take care of you no matter what life threw at us, and I meant every word. Trust me, baby. Trust us.
I love you always.
Preston

She read the note twice more and swallowed past the lump in her throat. She carefully set it on the bed next to her. The wrapping paper easily fell away from a small box with no pictures or wording on the outside. Mandy opened one end and reached inside. She gasped as she withdrew a silver picture frame with delicate filigree and butterflies etched all the way around.

Engraved at the bottom were the words, "Love. Hope. Family."

Mandy didn't realize she'd been crying until a tear splashed on her arm. She sniffed and used the sleeve of her nightshirt to dry her face.

He'd bought her a replacement frame for the photo of her grandparents. Preston's gift couldn't have been more perfect or thoughtful. Warmth filled her heart and radiated to every cell of her body.

That photo was still lodged in the broken frame. Mandy hadn't had the energy to do anything with it until now. She carefully took the back of the frame away and was surprised to see there were other pictures behind the first.

Mandy took the photo of her grandparents, intending to put it in the new frame. The picture below stopped her. She remembered the day Granny had asked Preston to take this picture of Mandy, Granny, and Papa on the front porch of the house. Mandy was seventeen and had gotten her driver's license. All three of them had big grins on their faces as they smiled at the camera and Preston behind it.

She ran a finger over the engraved words at the bottom of the new frame.

Love. When her parents signed over their parental rights and walked away, Mandy was nothing but a skinny, damaged kid with more problems than she could shake a stick at. Looking back now, she could see how God had never turned His back on her. He'd brought Papa and Granny into her life. They'd stepped up and given her the home and love she needed. If it hadn't been for them, Mandy had no idea what would have become of her.

And Preston. God had brought him into her life,

too. Preston loved her no matter how many times she'd pushed him away. Sure, he'd told her how he felt. He'd also shown her in more ways than she could count. She believed her heart had recognized his love, even when she refused to believe it before.

Hope. There'd been many times in her life when it would've been easy to lose hope. But every time she got close, God had reached down and given her a large enough dose to make it through. She hadn't realized it at the time, but looking back, she recognized the people in her life had shown her that hope was alive and well. That God was always there, even when she couldn't see Him. From Papa and Granny to Preston, from Ellen and Stanley to the amazing people at church, God continued to shower her with more blessings than she could count.

Family. God had provided Mandy with the family she needed. He'd given her Papa and Granny when her parents left her behind. And now? She had Preston.

She took their wedding photo out of the older frame and replaced it with the image of her, Granny, and Papa. With a soft smile, she touched Preston's face with one finger before putting their picture in the new frame.

She and Preston were a family. She sat in wonder as the love she'd ignored for far too long pushed its way to the surface. She loved Preston. Probably always had. She chuckled. Two people crazy enough to enter a marriage of convenience like they had deserved each other. She had to talk to him.

Mandy got dressed and cleaned up as quickly as possible. Disappointment doused her smile when she entered the living room and realized Preston wasn't home.

Ellen came in from the kitchen. When she saw Mandy's face, her own clouded with worry. "Is something wrong?"

"Where's Preston? I need to talk to him."

"He left early for the workshop."

Mandy was sure Preston had said yesterday he'd finished his work for the next couple of days. "What's going on, Ellen?" Her mother-in-law looked uncomfortable. "Please, tell me."

Ellen dried her hands on the towel she'd carried out with her. "Preston wanted to get quotes on the equipment in the workshop. He's hoping he can sell it and pay for repairs to your house."

"What? No! He can't do that. The business is his dream." Mandy ran into the bedroom and slipped her shoes on. She gave Ellen a hug on the way back through the living room. "We'll be back in a while." She barely registered the growing smile on Ellen's face as she closed the door behind her.

Once in her car, she dialed Preston's number. He answered on the second ring.

"Mandy? Is everything okay?"

"Are you at the workshop?"

"Yes. What's wrong?"

Mandy let out a sigh of relief. "I'm on my way. Please, don't sell anything until I get there."

"Mandy?" Preston sounded confused. She wasn't about to tell him any of this over the phone.

"I promise I'll tell you everything in person."

~*~

Preston stared at the phone after Mandy hung up as if he expected clarification.

Dad had offered to come with him this morning when Preston said he wanted to get quotes on the equipment. Selling it was the only thing he could think of to pay for the deductible for the house.

It was more important for him to make sure Mandy didn't lose the one thing that mattered most to her. That house reminded her of everything her grandparents stood for. Money would be tight, but he could help her with the websites and find another job in town. They'd make it work.

All that mattered was that they were together.

"Mandy's on her way here."

Dad looked confused. "Is everything okay?"

"She wouldn't talk to me on the phone." He dusted his hands off on his pants and headed outside to wait for her.

"I'll stay in here, son. You go on and talk to her."

Preston gave him a small smile and crossed the yard. He sat on the porch steps in front of the house, thankful for the shade the roof provided, and waited.

Mandy's car rolled up the driveway and stopped. She jumped out and ran to the stairs. "You didn't sell your equipment, did you?"

"What? No. I haven't even gotten quotes on the equipment yet." He stood and walked down the steps to join her. "Mom told you what I'm going to do, didn't she?" He motioned toward the workshop. "If we can sell it all, we should be able to pay for the deductible. Then we can get the house fixed for you."

"I don't want it fixed."

He blinked at her, half expecting her to tell him she was joking. But the way she was looking at him said she was serious. "What do you mean?"

"Look at it. The damage, it's too much." She

looked around her a few moments before meeting his gaze again. "If we sell this place and all the land, we could afford a house and a place for your business. Probably with money to spare."

Preston couldn't believe his ears. "But you love this place. It means everything to you."

"Not anymore." She took a step toward him, her stature radiating confidence.

Surely, she didn't fully grasp what she was saying. "It's the last connection you have to your grandparents. The legacy your family left you."

She shook her head. "That's just it, Preston. I've been so focused on the past that I grew up clinging to my life as if it could be taken away at any moment. But I realized something this morning. Every time I thought things were falling apart, God was holding my hand. Papa and Granny took me in when they didn't have to. They showed me God's love every day of their lives. Their example and the memories I hold are their legacy to me. Not the house." Her lips curved into a smile. "And God brought you into my life when I needed you most, even if I didn't realize it at the time." She chuckled. "You are my family, Preston."

His heart stalled as her words sank in. He reached out to touch her face with one hand.

She covered his with one of her own. "I'm sorry I took so long to see it. This house? The land? It's just a place. And you've been willing to give up everything to keep it for me. I can't let you do that. You've worked too hard for this business to let it go like that. This is your dream."

"No, you're my dream. And I'd sell all of this in a heartbeat if that's what made you happy."

"That's just it. *You* are what makes me happy. I

was stubborn, and I refused to see that for years." She squeezed his hand. "I love you, Preston. Honestly? I think I always have."

He searched her eyes, desperate for confirmation. The love and trust he saw reflecting back at him kicked his pulse into high gear as every doubt fled his mind. In one motion, he claimed her lips in a kiss expressing all the love and happiness he wanted to show her for the rest of their lives.

When he pulled back, he enjoyed seeing the pink in her cheeks and the way her lips appeared fuller and redder from his kisses. "It sure took you long enough." He smiled and gave her a wink.

She grinned as she tried to give him a playful shove. He dodged her hand and stepped to the side. It took little effort to snag her by the waist, pull her close, and hold both her hands in one of his. "I think I've got you now. What are you going to do about it?"

With a mischievous little quirk of her eyebrow, Mandy stood on tiptoes until her mouth was only a breath away from his. "This." She closed the gap in one of the sweetest kisses he'd ever known.

Two months later, Mandy and Preston stood in front of her grandparents' house. The last of the items salvaged from the fire had been removed a week ago. Thankfully, the photo albums kept in the cedar chest in the living room had come through the ordeal unscathed.

Mandy zipped up the front of her coat to keep out the cold January wind. The news said there was a possibility of snow later in the week. Even the air smelled like winter. She tilted her head slightly as she stared at the house. "Perspective is a weird thing."

Preston pulled the hood of his jacket up over his head and looked at her quizzically. "How so?"

"In September, my whole life was wrapped up in that house. Now? It's just an empty hull. I thought I'd be sad coming here and seeing it for the last time."

He moved behind her and put his arms around her waist. "And you're not?"

"Not really. I'm good with the company buying this land and turning it into a camp for families. I think Papa and Granny would love the idea of kids playing by the creek and chasing fireflies every summer."

"I think they would, too." He nuzzled her cheek.

Mandy giggled as his cold nose tickled her. "Besides, I can't wait to move into our new place next week." They'd found the perfect house on five acres of land only twenty minutes from church and fifteen minutes from his parents' place. This coming spring, they hoped to have a large metal building built on the property. For now, the oversized garage would be big enough to house the woodworking business.

"Me neither. Mom and Dad have been great about letting us stay with them." Preston turned her around in his arms until she faced him. "But I can't wait until we're in our own home." His lips brushed against her cheek. "And I have you all to myself."

This time, his warm lips covered hers. Everything around Mandy faded away as she melted in her husband's arms.

Epilogue

Two Years Later

Mandy drifted in and out of sleep. The beeps of the heart rate machine helped to drown some of the noise from outside her hospital room. Every cell in her body seemed drained of energy. The sudden sound of the blood pressure cuff accompanied the tightening band on her arm and broke into her moments of rest.

A noise at the doorway prompted Mandy to open her eyes. One of her nurses smiled at her. "Your guys should be back any minute now. You doing okay?"

"I am, thank you."

The nurse looked behind her and shifted out of the doorway. "Right on time. Come in."

The moment Preston appeared with the little blue bundle in his arms, all of Mandy's exhaustion faded away. She scooted herself up on the bed a little. "Hey! I missed you both. Everything go okay?"

"Are you kidding?" Preston sat on the edge of the bed and gazed at his infant son a moment before handing him over to Mandy. "They got him all cleaned up, and Barry here handled it like a champ." He lifted the hat a little to reveal soft swirls of hair. "Look how dark it is, even when it's dry."

She ran a finger over the strands and breathed in deep. Everything about their son was perfect, from his ten fingers and toes to the way he pursed his tiny lips. "He has your nose."

"You think so? I also see some of your family in his face. Doesn't he have your grandfather's chin?"

The possibility brought moisture to her eyes, and she blinked it away. "They'd be really proud that we named Barry after Papa."

"They sure would." Preston pressed a kiss to her forehead and another one to Barry's.

The baby shifted before releasing the sweetest little sigh. Mandy shook her head in amazement. "How is it possible to fall in love with someone you've just barely met?"

Preston shrugged. "All I know is that it's happened to me twice now." He winked and gave her a smile that melted her heart.

"Sometimes you say the sweetest things."

"It's a gift."

Mandy giggled. "I love you, Preston."

He stood so he could lean in and give her a proper kiss. "I love you, too, baby."

She smiled at him and marveled at how her life had turned out.

Praise God, Preston was right. Never say never.

Thank you!

I appreciate you for taking the time to read **Marrying Mandy**. I hope you enjoyed it and you'll consider leaving a review on Amazon and/or Goodreads. I like hearing what you think about it, and it'll help other readers discover new books as well.

If you enjoyed **Marrying Mandy**, you might enjoy my other marriage of convenience book, **Calming the Storm**. Also, keep your eyes out for Raven's story in the second book of the Brides of Clearwater.

Acknowledgments

Doug, I can never thank you enough for your support. Your belief in what I'm doing, the extra opportunities to write, and your encouragement make all the difference in the world. I love you!

As always, Crystal, your support as my friend and critique partner made this whole process that much easier. I'm so thankful to have someone I can bounce ideas off and who isn't afraid to tell me when I need to take a scene or plot point and chuck it out the window. Here's to tea, chocolate, and friendship. You rock, girl!

Krista, it was a pleasure to work with you on this book. Your editing was exactly what I needed to polish things up and get the story to where I wanted it to be. Thanks for taking care of my book baby. I look forward to working with you again in the future.

Thanks for the gorgeous work you did on the cover, Vicki. It turned out beautifully! Your encouragement, advice, and suggestions on this project as a whole were invaluable.

There's a lot that goes into writing a story that I'm proud to send out into the world. A big thank you to the members of my critique group, Rachel and Kris, who offered great suggestions. I'm also thankful for my beta readers: Denny, Steph, Suzanne (Mom), and Sandy. I appreciate you all!

More than anything else, I'm so grateful that God's given me the opportunity to not only do what I love, but to share my books with others. To Him be the glory!

About the Author

Melanie D. Snitker has enjoyed writing fiction for as long as she can remember. She started out creating episodes of cartoon shows she wanted to see as a child, and her love of writing grew from there. She and her husband live in Texas with their two children, who keep their lives full of adventure, and two dogs, who add a dash of mischief to the family dynamics. In her spare time, Melanie enjoys photography, reading, crocheting, baking, and hanging out with family and friends.

http://www.melaniedsnitker.com
https://twitter.com/MelanieDSnitker
https://www.facebook.com/melaniedsnitker

Subscribe to Melanie's newsletter and receive a monthly e-mail containing recipes, information about new releases, giveaways, and more! You can find a link to sign up on her website.

Books by Melanie D. Snitker

Calming the Storm
(A Marriage of Convenience)

Love's Compass Series:
Finding Peace (Book 1)
Finding Hope (Book 2)
Finding Courage (Book 3)
Finding Faith (Book 4)
Finding Joy (Book 5)
Finding Grace (Book 6)

Life Unexpected Series:
Safe In His Arms (Book 1)
Someone to Trust (Book 2)

Welcome to Romance
Finding Forever in Romance

Brides of Clearwater Series:
Marrying Mandy (Book 1)

Made in the USA
Monee, IL
02 April 2021

64495322R00115